JUNGLE OF GLASS

JUNGLE OF GLASS

The New Ed Rogan Mystery

Gerald J. Davis

To the Woods,

Dear friends of long standing.

Best Wishes,

Gerald J Davis

JULY 2005

Writer's Showcase
San Jose New York Lincoln Shanghai

Jungle of Glass
The New Ed Rogan Mystery

Writer's Showcase
an imprint of iUniverse, Inc.

For information address:
iUniverse, Inc.
5220 S. 16th St., Suite 200
Lincoln, NE 68512
www.iuniverse.com

ISBN: 0-595-23579-4

Printed in the United States of America

For Peter and Jennifer

Faithful are the wounds of a friend;
but the kisses of an enemy are deceitful.

—Proverbs 27:5-6

CHAPTER 1

She knocked on the outer door of my office. Three sharp raps. Christ, no one ever knocked on my door anymore. People just opened the door and barged right in. What ever happened to good old-fashioned common courtesy? Guess it went the way of carbon paper.

I debated whether to yell "Come in" or get up and open the door for her. She'd sounded like a real lady over the phone, so I got up.

I was right. When I opened the door, there stood the Czarina. Regal, she was.

And stunning, too.

She looked to be in her sixties. There was an air of cool superiority about her. Her face was finely-chiseled and her bone structure was superb. Her mouth was small and tightly-drawn. The eyes were large and luminous.

And she had been crying.

She just stood there in the hallway even though I held the door open for her.

"Please come in, Mrs. Roderick," I said.

She forced a grim smile and stepped past me into the outer office and stood there like a Botticelli image forty years later.

I let the outer door close by itself with a soft click and ushered her into my office. She surveyed the room with an obvious look of disdain. She didn't sit down until I offered her a chair, and she sat with a graceful movement that could have come from the stage. By the way she looked around, you could see she wasn't used to such cramped quarters. Her bathroom was probably bigger than the inner and outer offices put together.

She was wearing a full length black Russian sable coat that could've cost anywhere between a small fortune and a large fortune, depending on whether she'd bought it at the Salvation Army Store or Saks Fifth Avenue. December in New York can get pretty frigid, especially for someone from the tropics.

Without even a sideways glance, she shrugged off the gross domestic product of your average third-world country and tossed it over the ratty chair next to her. It was the kind of lazy gesture that's second nature to someone who doesn't often think about money.

I walked around the desk and dropped into my chair.

She sat there primly facing me, her back straight as a flagpole, her hands interlocked in her lap, her knees tight together. She could have been a statue.

I tried to lighten the atmosphere.

"Would you like a martini or a banana daiquiri, Mrs. Roderick?"

There was a small fixed smile on her lips. The smile extended another millimeter on each side. "Mr. Rogan, it is nine o'clock in the morning. I hope you are attempting a little humor." Her voice was a little softer than you'd expect from her appearance. She didn't have an accent, but there was a tone that said English wasn't her first language.

I leaned back. "Yup, that's what it was. A note of levity to make you feel more comfortable."

She fixed her gaze on me and I had the feeling she'd done it many times before with a misbehaving servant. "There is no need for such an effort, Mr. Rogan." She straightened her neck even more and stuck out her chin. "I am a strong woman."

She sure gave that impression. Her hair, which showed traces of the original strawberry blond, and which was now mostly defiantly white, was drawn back severely in a bun. Her skin was flawless, except for those tiny wrinkles around the mouth and eyes. She'd obviously had a facelift or two. It was a clear demonstration of what a little cash can do for your appearance.

She wanted to get to the point, so I let her. "Go ahead, Mrs. Roderick. Tell me what the problem is."

Then she surprised me. This royal creature lost her composure. She burst out crying. Or should I say bawling. She sobbed like a six year old girl, her chest heaving and her breath coming in short gasps.

I kept a box of Kleenex in the lower right hand drawer of the desk next to the Old Bushmill for just such a contingency. So I opened the drawer, eyed the whisky, took out the box and shoved it across the metal desktop toward her. She probably would have been embarrassed if I had done any more.

She ignored the tissues and used her own handkerchief. It was silk with delicate lace embroidery that didn't do a good job of drying her tears. She kept on sobbing for a couple of minutes. I didn't know what to do, so I got up and went to the outer office and got her a cup of Polish Water from the cooler.

I gave her the water. As I did, I caught a whiff of her perfume. It was faint, understated. The scent reminded you of a meadow of blossoms on a sunny summer afternoon.

She took a sip, and from the way she held it, it was evident she wasn't used to drinking from paper cups.

Finally she pulled herself together, took another sip, and handed the cup back to me. I tossed it into the basket, water and all.

"I'm sorry, Mr. Rogan," she said and I could see she meant it. I would have bet even money she hadn't cried since primary school when some smart-alec boy had twisted her arm.

She pulled herself forward and sat on the edge of her chair. Her eyes looked deep into mine as she took my measure.

"Mr. Rogan," she said. "I called you because Mr. Jim Broadbent said you were a man of confidence." She had translated the expression directly from the Spanish.

I nodded but didn't say anything.

"Mr. Broadbent said I could rely on you." She put her fingertips on the edge of the desk. They were perfectly manicured and the polish was a flaming red. It was the only thing about her that was overstated. "My husband has been kidnapped."

"That's not a job for me. The FBI handles kidnappings. You have to talk to them."

She shook her head. "No, no. The kidnapping happened in El Salvador."

"What about the local authorities?" I knew what the answer would be.

She rolled her eyes. "The local authorities have begun working on this matter but I do not have a high level of confidence in their ability to find my husband"…she paused…"alive."

"But why come to me in New York? You…"

She cut me off. "The ransom note was mailed from New York to my flat in New York." She opened her large Hermes pocketbook, fished around for a minute and came up with a plain white number ten envelope.

"Here it is," she said as she handed it to me. She held it between her thumb and forefinger as if it reeked to high heaven with some foul poison.

The postmark said December tenth. Four days ago. It had been stamped at the main post office at Thirty-third Street and Eighth Avenue. There was a regular first-class stamp. Nothing else on the envelope except her address. I knew the building. Fifth at Eighty-second. Across from the museum. It was a very elegant address.

How long did it take a letter to get across town? Two days? Three?

I shook the letter out of the envelope and opened it by the edges. "Did you have a lab check this?"

She gave me a blank look.

The letter was on plain bond paper. Times Roman typeface on a laser printer.

PUTA

TU ESPOSO MORIRA DE MALA FORMA SI NO NOS ENTRE-GAS CINCO MILLIONES DE DOLARES EN EFFECTIVO EN BILLETES DE NO MAS DE CIEN DOLARES. ESPERA NUES-TRAS INSTRUCCIONES.

ATLACATL.

The salutation was somewhat less than cordial. It threatened her husband with an unpleasant death unless these miscreants got five million dollars in small denominations.

I didn't get the closing. "What is Atlacatl?" I asked her.

'It is the name of an Indian chief of long ago."

"And what relevance does it have now?"

There was a flash behind her eyes. "I do not know. It has no meaning to me."

"When was your husband kidnapped?"

"Four days ago-on the tenth of December."

"The same day the letter was postmarked?"

She nodded. "Yes."

"Where were you when it happened?"

"I was in New York."

I looked into her large coffee-brown eyes. "Do you live in New York?"

She stuck out her jaw. "*We* live in El Salvador."

"But…"

"We have homes in several locations-New York, Miami, El Salvador, Ireland."

"Ireland?"

She nodded grimly. "Yes. My husband is the Honorary Consul for Ireland."

"But you were here and he…"

"My husband's business…"

"They knew you were here."

She gave a short nod. "They know a lot."

Then she fell silent.

I was about to ask her another question when she said, "Will you handle this matter for me?"

My smile was as reassuring as I could make it. I tried to add some warmth for effect. "I took the case when I first heard your voice on the phone."

Her smile was bittersweet. "Mr. Rogan, you are very gallant." She put the accent on the last syllable.

"That's what all my ex-wives used to say."

She got up. "How much is your fee?"

It was a smooth segue. She'd put me in my place, which was obviously not quite on her level. Talk is cheap.

"Five hundred a day plus expenses."

Without a blink, she pulled out her checkbook and wrote me a check. She wrote with one of those oversized fountain pens with a gold nib and it made a scratching sound as she scribbled out a lot of zeros.

She handed it to me. The check was for twenty grand.

Either she was being overly generous or she didn't think I was Sam Spade.

The check was drawn on Morgan Private Banking. I knew I wouldn't have to call the bank to see if the check was good.

CHAPTER 2

The TACA flight left Miami at two-thirty seven the next afternoon. I took American Airlines non-stop to Miami and then it was direct to the new airport an hour outside San Salvador. Ilopango, the old airport, was now being used for military aviation.

Transportes Areos de Centro America had never inspired much of a feeling of confidence in me. Travelers had a sardonic habit of referring to it as "bota tuercas" which meant "dropping screws."

Good thing I was a fatalist.

There was no movie going down so I read a copy of the ransom note over and over between chapters of a tourist guide to El Salvador. Mrs. Roderick had filled me in on the details of the kidnapping, or as much as she knew. But the only way to get the feel of it was to be boots on the ground.

The stewardesses in their freshly-pressed navy blue uniforms were friendly, polite and accommodating, unlike the help on some domestic airlines I could name. They tried to make the best of the rudimentary amenities on the ancient 707. They served me a meal loosely referred to as steak, but it would've been much easier to chew on a Kevlar crotch protector. At least I was able to wash it down with a passable version of the local brew.

The flight landed in the middle of a late-afternoon downpour. It didn't seem to bother the crew much, so I didn't let it bother me.

Besides, these jockeys could land a C5-A on a floating cork in the middle of a hurricane. And most of them had been flying longer than I cared to remember.

The airport was modern and sterile. I passed through immigration and customs quickly. Nobody asked me about the Glock 9mm that was tucked neatly between the skivvies and the socks at the bottom of my suitcase, or maybe they were just too fastidious to go rooting about in the middle of a person's intimate garments.

I stepped outside the glassed-in reception area into a blast of tropical air that hit me in the face like a hot thick wet blanket. A cabby pulled up in front of me, but I didn't like his lean and hungry look so I waved him on and pointed to the next car in line. It was a rickety ten-year old gray Toyota without air-conditioning and there were more dents in it than the loser of a demolition derby. The driver was a little guy with a scraggly mustache and a smile that never left his face. He told me his name was Luis and that he'd be glad to be my driver while I was in country. I told him he had a deal. In any case, it was cheaper than renting a car and I wouldn't have to waste my time folding and unfolding tourist maps.

The ride in from the airport was humid and dusty. We passed desolate stretches of vegetation interspersed with shantytowns of tin-roofed shacks and open sewers. The rain had stopped but this was the dry season, or summer as the locals called it, and the landscape was arid and brown.

The shocks on this so-called taxi had completely given out who knows how many years ago and my head kept hitting the roof of the goddam car, sending little twinges down my spine and bringing unspoken curses to my mouth. The road was so full of potholes it looked like someone had shelled this stretch of the countryside.

I leaned forward. "Luis, tell me. Have you heard about the kidnapping of the honorary consul?"

"Si, Senor." He spoke as he stared straight ahead. "All the world has heard of it."

I stared at the bald spot on the back of his head. "And who do the people say are responsible?"

He shrugged. "A saber. There are many rumors. Some say the leftists, some say the criminals…"

"And what is your opinion?"

He shook his head. "In this country it is best to have no opinion."

Short and sweet. I grinned at the back of his head.

As we got closer to the city, more and more people appeared by the side of the road. When we finally reached the outskirts of San Salvador, there were masses of people everywhere. The sea of humanity was overwhelming. Just wave after wave of sad bastard souls ground down by the condition of simply being human in an underdeveloped country.

"Luis," I said as I leaned forward and talked into his ear, "Tell me, which is the best beer?"

He turned all the way around to grin at me, oblivious of the road. "Senor, without a doubt Suprema."

I'd made a reservation at the Camino Real to be close to the US embassy. By the time we got to the hotel, I was sweating like a water buffalo in a mud hole and very thirsty to boot.

"Luis," I said. "Do me the honor of joining me in the bar for a drink."

He turned around again. His eyes had brightened and his grin showed a gap where a couple of teeth should have been. "Si, Senor. You do me a great honor." Tentatively, he extended his hand over the back of his seat. I took it. His hand was small and rough, but his grip was dry and firm.

We got out of the car. I put my hand on his shoulder. He looked up at me. I was about three times its height.

"Leave the bag in the car," I said. "I have a great thirst." I grabbed my suit jacket from the car and slung it over my shoulder.

We walked through the lobby of the hotel and turned left into the lounge. It was dark and cool and almost empty. There were a couple of Americans at the bar who I took to be reporters, or even lower forms of life.

The bar could have been in Singapore, Johannesburg or Rio. It was the same demented interior decorator at work in every hotel in the free world and selected locations in the former second world. If you had gone to sleep and just opened your eyes, you wouldn't have known where in the world you were. To paraphrase a former Vice President of Greek extraction, you seen one hotel, you seen them all.

Luis followed me to a small table in the corner with a view of the doorway. The waiter was there before we sat down. I was impressed. The bar was a good-sized room and the guy had a long distance to traverse.

"Luis, what will you have?"

He stuck up his index finger. "Una Suprema."

"Dos Supremas, por favor," I said.

I put my elbows on the table and looked at Luis' face. He couldn't have been more than forty but his face was deeply lined. There was a quiet dignity in his eyes.

"Tell me, if I wanted to find out more about the kidnapping who should I talk to?"

He dropped his gaze and spread his hands on the table. They were dirty and callused. "Senor, you should speak to Adolfo, the chauffeur."

"Can you take me to him?"

He nodded. "Si, Senor. The cousin of my wife lives across the street from his house."

"Excellent," I said. "We'll see him tomorrow. Today I want to go to the embassy of the United States."

"Senor, the embassy is closed. It is too late."

"Very well," I said. "Tonight we drink. Tomorrow we go to the embassy."

CHAPTER 3

I went down to dinner at eight-ten that night. I'd showered and changed and called Jim Broadbent at home to set up a meeting at nine the next morning. Broadbent wasn't there so I left a message with his maid and hoped she'd remember to tell him.

The dining room of the hotel was half-full, mostly with locals, from what I could tell. Almost everybody was smoking and a blue haze hung over the room. No point in asking for the no-smoking section. If they had one, it was probably located in Milwaukee.

No more than half a second after I sat down, a guy slid into the chair across from me and pulled it up to the table.

"Mind if I join you?" he said in English.

I shrugged. "How can I mind a *fait accompli?*"

He was one of the characters I'd seen drinking at the bar that afternoon. Thin and sallow with a stubbly beard that looked about a week old. His hair was a little too long. His voice had the rough edge that came from too many shots of bourbon at too many late night jazz joints.

He stuck out his hand. "Gene McInerny. Or Eugene O'Neill McIn-erny, if you want the whole moniker." His voice had a real lilt to it, like he was happy to be living. He wore wire-rimmed aviator glasses and a purple Ralph Lauren Polo shirt.

I shook his hand. "Ed Rogan."

"I'm a freelancer."

I grinned at him. "Isn't everybody?"

He laughed. His voice was deep, but when he laughed, it became high pitched. "No, I mean I'm a freelance reporter—a stringer. I write for the *Times*, the *New Yorker*, *Atlantic Monthly*, and any other pinko rag that would actually be willing to pay me for my worthless verbiage."

"Ever try the *National Review*?"

He shook his head. "Naw, I tried it once but I couldn't bring myself to do it. It's not my slant. I've been in and out of Salvador for ten years, mostly writing about the civil war. Now that it's over I've been bored out of my mind, so I've taken to drinking myself into a stupor every night."

"Sounds like an honorable pastime," I said.

"That's why I was so pleased when you showed up."

"You don't say."

"You're here to investigate the kidnapping, right?"

"What makes you say that?"

His eyes gleamed like he'd just found a dime bag of Panama Red. "Listen, man. This burg's been dead for months. Dullsville, you get my drift. All of a sudden, praise the Lord, we get this super story—an international snatch. And then the rumors are flying around that a hot shot private investigator is on his way and then you show up looking like old Philip Marlowe in the flesh."

"What makes you thing it's international?" I asked him.

He squinted at me. "You Jewish?"

I grunted. "Why do you say that?"

"Why do you keep answering a question with another fucking question?"

"Hell, you just did it too," I said.

He spread his hands in the air. "I give up. Ream me with somebody else's dick. You got me. Status quo ante bellum, OK?"

I shrugged. "OK. What's your angle?"

"It's like this," he said. "You investigate the case. I profile you for the mass media. I make you into a superstar. Your business grows exponentially. You get rich. You get to bang any broad you want. They come swarming around you like bees to honey."

"It's flies to honey," I said.

"I'm not too good on metaphors. My long suit is insightful reporting." He looked at me. "Well, what do you say?"

"What's in it for you?"

He hesitated for a moment. "I get a story with a different angle. The kidnapping is just a story. Everyone's writing about it the same way. You're the twist that differentiates the story. Lochinvar from out of the West, you know. The hero who saves the day."

The waiter came over to the table and stood next to me.

"Beer?" I asked McInerny.

He shook his head slowly. "Flor de Cana for me," he said.

"How can you drink that swill?"

His grin widened. "It's better than absinthe. It rots the brain twice as fast."

"You one of those self-destructive reporter stereotypes?"

"I commend you on your acuity," he said.

I ordered a Suprema for myself and a Flor de Cana for McInerny. The waiter gave me a slight bow, a curt "Si, Senor" and backed away from us.

"Listen, Mac," I said. "I want information. You give me information, I'll give you a story. Quid pro quo."

His smile became diabolical. "A gentleman of great judgment and wisdom. I think this is the start of a beautiful friendship."

"He's literary, too," I said.

"Screenplays are not literary."

"Have it your way," I shrugged. "Tell me what you know about the kidnapping."

The waiter came back with our drinks and placed them very carefully on little coasters on the table, as if he was handling some plutonium cocktail. I took a swig of beer. McInerny tossed back his head and gulped the foul liquid without a grimace.

"It happened at high noon on the doble via—the Avenida Franklin Delano Roosevelt, for you gringos," he said. "It never should have happened."

"What do you mean?"

He took another gulp of his drink. This time he did grimace. "Roderick was riding in a Range Rover that had more armor-plating than a fucking Abrams tank. One car with the kidnappers was in front of him—one car with kidnappers was behind him. They boxed him in. But there was no way they could've gotten to him. He could've just sat there till the Fiesta de Agosto."

The waiter reappeared silently and asked very softly and politely if we wished to order. I hadn't even opened the menu. But I was hungry.

"Give me a steak," I said. "Medium rare."

McInerny shook his head. "Bad choice," he said to me. To the waiter he said, "Give my friend the fish."

"I don't like fish," I said.

"All the more reason. The steaks come from malnourished cows that look like they're about to drop dead."

"What else do they have?"

"The shrimp is good. Real tasty and as big as your loblolly."

"Then they must be big shrimp," I said. I took another slug of beer. "OK, I'll buy that."

"Dos camarones del rio," McInerny said to the waiter. "And another round of drinks."

He turned back to me. "You want to know how they grabbed him? The driver's the key. Either he panicked or he was in on it."

"Why?"

His eyes narrowed. "The driver opened the goddam door and got out. That's how the kidnappers got in and grabbed our Mr. Roderick. El Gordo."

"He was fat?"

He shook his head. "Nah. It's an idiom. Don't take it so literally. It means the jackpot, the prize."

I nodded. "The police question the driver?"

McInerny snorted. "Listen, Rogan. Everybody's got an agenda here. The police want to pin it on the left, the left want to pin it on the military, the military want to pin it on the politicians, the politicians want to pin it on the criminals."

"So, who did it?"

He spread his hands palms up. "As they say here—a saber." He looked at me for a long time. "You remember what Churchill said about Russia?"

"Yeah," I nodded. "A riddle wrapped in an enigma surrounded by a mystery."

"It's like that here," he said. "Only worse. When you think you know what it is—it's not it."

CHAPTER 4

It was early in the morning but the day was already stifling. The shirt was sticking to my back so I decided to forget the suit jacket. I opened the collar button and loosened my tie.

I stood in front of the Camino Real waiting for Luis.

I had told him to pick me up at a quarter to nine. He showed up at nine thirty-five. Not bad for Tropical Standard Time.

The embassy was a five minute drive from the hotel. In front of the multi-tiered fortress-like building was a redondel with some half-dead flowers in the middle and vendors selling vegetables and pupusas around the perimeter. There was a tall fence of iron bars around the compound and the three-story white building in the middle but it wasn't nearly enough to protect the people inside against fifty-caliber machine gun rounds or a shoulder-launched rocket. And there were signs of a halfhearted attempt to cover the battle scars on the facade of the building.

In front of the embassy was a line of locals that snaked all the way around the block like they were giving away fifty-dollar bills.

The Marine guard at the entrance wouldn't let Luis park there to wait for me. Part of the painfully-learned lessons of one too many car bombs and the ghosts of the people who died in the embassy bombings and the Khobar Towers.

I told Luis to come back for me in an hour. As I passed the Marine, I snapped off a salute out of force of habit. There was a Salvadoran girl behind the reception desk in the large spare lobby. She was wearing a flowered dress and she had a small pink flower in her hair. She wrote out a pass, gave me a sweet smile and pointed to the elevator that would take me to Broadbent's office on the second floor.

I took the stairs instead. He was waiting for me outside his office with the same ear-to-ear grin I'd left him with in Chile years ago.

"Hello, Rogan," he said, as he gave me an abrazo. "How's your hammer hangin'?"

"Same as always, Jim. Only a little lower."

I stepped back to take a look at him. He'd aged a lot. Some people age rapidly, like they're burning up all their reserves. Some people don't age at all. What little hair he had was practically gone. So he shaved the rest.

I knew his age. He was only fifty.

He was large and heavy, with a bullet head, a square jaw and that loopy grin. His nose was slightly askew, and he walked with the movements of the boxer he was in his youth at Dartmouth.

He was ostensibly Commercial Attache here just like he was in Chile. Sure, it was a demotion, and I knew why. You can't go around banging the Ambassador's wife with impunity.

The woman in question, a charming hostess and an asset to any diplomat's career, had never had an orgasm before she met Broadbent. When he was busted for lascivious carriage and the Ambassador called in his markers to have Broadbent transferred to Paraguay, the Ambassador's wife, crazed by lust, demanded that they move to Paraguay, Paraguay for chrissake, but saner heads prevailed. The gray-haired men convinced her that her husband's career was more important than her orgasms. So much for the ways of the world.

Broadbent led me into his office and pulled up a chair for me. "Sit down, big guy," he said.

I sat down, leaned back and crossed my legs. "Whatever happened to Madame Ambassador?"

He moved his big frame behind his desk, sat down and waved his hand in a grand gesture. "She entered the pantheon of all-time outstanding lays."

Broadbent was known as a swordsman and the odds were good that he was still actively dueling. Parry and thrust, parry and thrust.

"Why did you send Mrs. Roderick to me?" I asked.

He put the palms of his hands on his face and rubbed his eyes, then slid his hands over his bald pate. "I figured you were as good as anybody in New York. Maybe better. Want to know how this is going to play out?"

"Sure."

"The family pays the ransom. Roderick is released. The whole thing is over in ten days."

"The family have any trouble raising the cash?"

He shook his head. "Hell, no. It's walking around money for them."

"What is Atlacatl?"

His eyebrows went up. "What?"

I repeated. "What is Atlacatl?"

"What the hell does that have to do with anything?"

"What does it mean?"

"It's the name of the Army's elite combat unit. But I don't see…"

"Tell me about Roderick," I said.

Broadbent got up and went over to the window. He pulled back a drape and looked out at the sun-washed street. A shaft of sunlight fell across the top of his desk, illuminating his In box like the beam of a spotlight.

"He's a remarkable man. An institution, really. And impressive to look at, too. A big man, raw bones, and a full head of red hair. The guy really stands out in this country where everyone's five-five and dark hair. And a royal son of a bitch, to boot. A lot of enemies over the years. His father came over from Ireland on a freighter that docked off the port of La Libertad. One night, his father got drunk and jumped ship because of some real or imagined slight. I disremember why. Roderick must have told me the story half a dozen times at cocktail parties, but I was too sloshed to remember now."

He went over to his desk, opened the top drawer and dropped a manila folder on my lap.

"I made up a file for you. It's all in there. Anyway, his father sent back to Ireland, to the old county, for a bride, like they did in those days. Roderick was born in El Salvador. Grew up here. Took over his father's finca—coffee farm to you—started other businesses, stores, factories, et cetera. Anyway, he became one of the richest men in the country. And he became the Honorary Consul of Ireland about ten years ago."

"That why he was grabbed?" I asked. "Does this have anything to do with the Provisional IRA or the Ulster Defense League?"

"I don't know…we don't know," he said, with a sigh.

"Is he Protestant or Catholic?"

"Never thought about it." He scratched his head. "Catholic, I guess."

"What do you think?" I asked him.

"You singular or you plural?"

I grinned at him. Ostensibly he was the Commercial Attache. But in Chile he was the CIA Station Chief and we worked together on a couple of hard cases when I was in security for ITT during that time when it was just a little more nasty than your friendly local telephone company. *Reach out and destabilize someone.* He was probably Station Chief here also.

"That's a shortcoming of the English language," I said. "We'll have to get the political correctness experts to come up with a plural You that isn't sexist."

He looked at me like I had two noses. When you're overseas for any length of time, you miss out on all the fun nuances of stateside life. "Both," I said. "Singular you and plural you."

He gave me a shrug. "Personally, I think the Left did it. Plural, we have no opinion."

"But you're looking into it?"

"Nope," he said. "None of our business. Doesn't affect our national interest one way or the other."

"Then how did I get into this?"

He rubbed his face again. "Personal matter. I felt sorry for Mrs. Roderick. I wanted to help her."

"You think it's political?"

"There's less of it now since the civil war wound down. But this is the kind of thing that used to happen all the time. Maybe old habits die hard."

Broadbent leaned forward and stared at me, as if he wanted to say something. Finally, he said, "There's one more thing. Roderick has a heart condition. He takes medication for it. You better find him and get him back to his family before the medication runs out."

CHAPTER 5

❀

At one o'clock that afternoon Luis drove me to a dusty part of town called Mejicanos. To call it a lower middle-class neighborhood would have been kind. Cobblestone streets gave way to dirt roads. The little Toyota humped along like a real trooper, but it was tough on the kidneys.

The fronts of the houses were crumbling and in need of serious repair. It was even hotter here than the other part of San Salvador where the hotel was, if that was possible. Hot and dusty. No wonder the beer monopoly was a gold mine.

We kept bouncing over rutted streets until Luis pulled up onto the sidewalk in front of a house with a small rusted Coca-Cola sign next to the front door. There was a Policia Nacional car parked on the corner half a block away. Two cops were sitting in the car. The cop in the passenger seat turned around, took a look at us, then turned back again.

Luis got out of the car, walked around it and opened the door for me.

"Luis," I said. "You do not have to do that. I am not an old lady."

"Si, Senor. It is only a gesture of courtesy."

"It is not necessary."

"Si, Senor. At your orders."

We stood on the cracked sidewalk in the midday heat and Luis pointed at a house across the street. "That is the house of my wife's cousin."

I nodded at him. "I see. Very well then, let us talk to the driver."

Luis knocked on the door. It was made of heavy wood and painted a pastel green. There was a shuffling sound inside and a middle-aged woman wearing an apron opened the door slowly. She looked at us without expression as Luis explained to her that I was a visitor from the United States on an important mission and that I wished to speak to Senor Alvarenga.

The woman nodded and said in a matter-of-fact way, "Imagine, Sir, it is like this. The Policia Nacional have been here and the Army have been here. They asked my husband many questions, which he answered completely and truthfully. Then yesterday he told me he was going to the store to buy cigarettes. But he never returned to the house. I waited all day and all night, but he never returned. I have much fear for his safety." She folded her fleshy arms over the apron to emphasize her words.

"Was this unusual behavior for your husband?" I asked her.

She studied me for a long time. There was no fear in her eyes, only a kind of resignation. "Yes," she said finally. "My husband is a good man. He slept at home every night. I have much fear." She was one of those stolid women I had seen so often in Latin America, decent, hard-working, uncomplaining.

"You think something bad happened to your husband?" I said.

She nodded impassively.

"You think someone took him?"

"Si, Senor," she said.

"Who do you think took him?"

Her large brown eyes closed slightly. "A saber? Who knows?"

"How long did your husband work for Sr. Roderick?"

"My husband was the chauffeur of Don Jaime for seventeen years." She drew a deep breath and stuck out her chin. "My husband never missed one day of work in seventeen years."

"Very commendable, Senora. But tell me what happened the day of the kidnapping."

We were still standing in the doorway of the house. The woman kept looking behind us into the street as if she couldn't make up her mind whether to ask us in or not.

"It was like any other day, Senor. My husband got up at the usual time, five o'clock. I got up and made breakfast for him, as always. He left for work at six, as always."

"How did he get to work?"

For the first time, she showed a sign of discomfort. She blinked. Then she blinked again.

"Our car was in the garage for repairs. So Don Jaime let my husband drive the Rover home." She pronounced it Rober, like Robert in French. "That was the auto he drove to work that day."

"What kind of car do you have?" I asked.

"We have a Morris." She pronounced it Maurice.

"And your car is back home now?"

"Si, Senor. It is fixed and we have it at home."

I nodded and signaled to Luis that it was time to go. "Many thanks, Senora Alvarenga," I said. "I hope your husband returns home soon in good health."

She showed no emotion. "Thank you, Senor. I pray to God this comes to pass."

Luis and I left and headed back to the car. "One moment," I said to Luis. "Is your wife's cousin home?"

"I think so," he said. "He is always home. He is very old."

"Can you take me to talk to him?"

"Si, Senor. Why not?"

He walked diagonally across the street and banged on the door so loud it sounded like he was Thor come to wreak vengeance on the unworthy. The house looked like the one we had just left, except that it was painted a long-faded blue. A girl came to the door. She wasn't more than twenty. She had a pert face with dark hair, dark skin, dark eyes and the look of a peasant.

She stared blankly at me but her eyes opened when she saw Luis.

"Don Luis," she said in a soft voice. "It is a surprise to see you."

"Si, Caridad," Luis said. He pointed at me. "This is Senor Rogan. He is my employer."

She smiled at me. A soft smile.

I inclined my head slightly. "With much pleasure, Senorita Caridad."

"Come inside," she said to both of us. "Don Jose is taking his siesta, but I will awaken him. He will be pleased to see you. No one comes to see him anymore."

We stepped into a modest living room. From the street, the place looked like a hovel, but inside it was an acceptable middle-class home, with a stereo, TV and VCR. So much for external appearances.

"Excuse me for a short moment," Caridad said. She left us alone in the room. It was reasonably cool inside the house, in contrast to the blast furnace outside on the street. The floors were tile and they dissipated the heat, or if that wasn't the reason, it was some other useful theory of thermal dissipation.

"Caridad is the housekeeper of my wife's cousin," Luis said to me by way of explanation. Then he gave me an opaque wink and said, "Don Jose is eighty and Caridad is twenty."

"I see," I said, for no reason.

A few minutes later, a short man in bare feet padded into the room. He was shorter than Caridad, but his shoulders were broad and he was powerfully built. He was wearing only a white undershirt and white boxer shorts, so you could see his bow legs. He had a full head of closely-cropped white hair and a thick white mustache. He gave Luis a broad smile when he saw him. There were a couple of teeth missing from the front of his mouth.

"Don Luis," he said with a booming voice. They hugged and slapped each other smartly on the back. Luis brought him over to me. "Don Jose, I am going to present to you Senor Rogan. He is my employer."

Don Jose gave me a hearty handshake. His grip was still strong. "It is a great pleasure to welcome you to my house." He clapped his hands loudly in the air. "Caridad," he said. "Bring us three beers."

This was a guy I could relate to.

He waved us to a wicker sofa and sat across from us in a wicker armchair with thick cushions. Within a couple of minutes Caridad came back into the room with three bottles of Pilsener and three iced glasses on a wooden tray. She served them to us with a small smile, taking care to pour the brew slowly down the side of the tilted glass, and then she quietly left the room.

"How can I be of service to you?" the old man said.

"Don Jose," I said. "I am investigating the kidnapping of Senor Roderick."

"I understand," he said gravely and stared into my eyes. "And how can I help in this matter?"

"Senor Roderick's chauffeur lives across the street."

He nodded slowly.

"Tell me what you can about this man and his habits."

Don Jose looked straight ahead at a point over my shoulder. I had the feeling he was composing his thoughts. His gaze was steady and serene.

"Look, Senor," he said finally. "I have known Senor Alvarenga for many years. He is a good man. He does not drink and does not gamble or go to the whores. He works hard. He has a good position. He has been the chauffeur of Senor Roderick for many years. Once, many years ago, I saw him drunk. He had much shame for that and I never saw him drunk again. That is what I know about Senor Alvarenga." He sat back in his armchair and took a drink of his beer.

"Thank you very much, Don Jose, for your information," I said. "Can you tell me if you noticed anything different about Senor Alvarenga or his family recently?"

He nodded. "I am an old man. I do not sleep very well. Sometimes, in the middle of the night, I walk around the house. Twice, while I stood here in the living room in the dark looking out at the street, I have seen men going into Senor Alvarenga's house."

"And who were these men?"

He rubbed the gray stubble on his chin. "This I cannot say."

"How many men were there?" I asked him. "What did they look like?"

"Senor, the street is not lit at night. There is a street light on the corner, but it has not been lit for many months, so it is difficult to answer your question. Once, there were three men. The other time there were five. More than that I cannot say."

"They were wearing regular street clothing?"

His jaw tightened and he looked at Luis. "Si, Senor. I believe so."

I got up. "Thank you, Don Jose, for your hospitality."

We shook hands. Caridad appeared out of nowhere and led us to the door.

"May you travel well," she said, almost in a whisper.

"Many thanks, Senorita Caridad," I said.

As we stepped out into the blinding mid-afternoon sunlight, Luis said, "Was Don Jose of help to you?"

"More than he knows," I said.

CHAPTER 6

❀

When I got back to the Camino Real, there was a note waiting for me. It was in a perfectly-formed female handwriting inviting me to dinner that evening at eight. The note was written in English and signed Marta Roderick.

"Where is San Benito?" I asked Luis.

"It is the colony with the biggest houses."

I showed him the note. "I have been invited to dinner tonight. Do you know this address?"

"Si, Senor. It is the house of Senor Roderick."

His grin was full of lust. "Senor, you are a lucky man. Nina Marta is a beautiful woman."

"We'll see about that, Luis." I winked at him. "Beautiful women don't affect me."

"We shall see, Senor," he said. "If this is true, you are not a real man."

"Pick me up at seven forty-five. Then we will see."

I went up to my room and called a number Broadbent had given me. Broadbent had said this man was a colonel in the army who would be helpful. The colonel wasn't there so I left my name and number and a message to call me.

I didn't know what else to do before dinner. I flopped down on the rack, turned on the TV and switched around the dial until I got

CNN. There was a segment about the best chocolate-chip cookie, which turned out to come from Bloomingdale's and which cost two bucks apiece. Two bucks for one goddam cookie. That was the daily wage for the average laborer in this country. One day's hard labor for a cookie. Go ahead and try to figure the economics of that equation.

I kicked off my shoes and propped a pillow against the headboard. The hum of the air-conditioning was enough to knock me out. Inside of two minutes I was sleeping the sleep of the untroubled.

❀   ❀   ❀

The phone woke me. I looked at my watch. It was ten to six.

"This is Colonel Mayorga. What can I do for you?" The voice was softly sibilant and oddly soothing.

"Jim Broadbent of the US embassy gave me your name. He said you might be able to help me in an urgent matter."

"Of course," he said. "I understand. When can we meet?"

"I'll be busy from eight to about eleven tonight. Can you meet me after that?"

"Certainly." His voice had the distinctive Salvadoran accent, but he lisped so it sounded like he came from Spain. "Can we meet at eleven-thirty?"

"Sure," I said. "Where?"

"Do you know the Hotel El Salvador?"

"I can find it."

"Good. I will meet you in the hotel parking lot."

"How will I know you?"

"Don't worry," he said. "I will know you."

He hung up.

CHAPTER 7

The address was on Avenida las Acacias in one of the most expensive parts of town. The house itself was half the size of a small town and the grounds were three times as big. It stood far back from the street at the end of a softly-sloping rise behind a ten-foot brick wall with cut glass embedded in the cement on top. The cut glass wasn't there to keep the birds off.

The style was modern with Spanish influences, but it was kind of jarring. Like the Naked Maja in a thong bikini.

It cost Luis the better part of a gas tank to drive all the way from the front gate to the steps of the house. A maid in starched whites swung open the oversized wooden door all by herself and led me down a long corridor to the sala. The house was a quadrangle with an open atrium in the center. The atrium had a large garden with lots of brightly-colored tropical flowers that you could see through glass walls. The only plant I could name was a Bird of Paradise.

Luis was right about Marta. She was a good-looking woman. And she did have an effect on me. But to tell you the truth, she wasn't as good-looking as her mother. There must have been too much of her father's rough-hewn Irish heritage that coarsened her mother's delicate features.

As the maid led me into the sala, Marta came to greet me. She had a head of angry red hair, full and long, and flashing blue-gray eyes.

There were freckles across the bridge of her nose. She had a strong jaw and bright even teeth. She looked to be in her late twenties. She was wearing a dressing gown that hung open because she hadn't bothered to tie it up. It didn't look like the kind of dress you wore to a dinner party.

"Mr. Rogan," she said as she walked up two steps to where I was standing and gave me her hand. "I didn't expect you so early." She was a tall girl, and she wasn't bashful about her height.

"Your invitation said eight."

She laughed. It was a hearty laugh. Nothing feminine about it. "Yes. But here, eight means nine."

I shrugged. "I'm a gringo. To me eight means eight."

"And you're wearing a suit."

"I always wear a suit. It's my work uniform."

"You will find it is uncomfortable to wear a suit in the tropics. You will sweat like a stuck pig."

"I learn by experience," I said. "Sometimes I learn the hard way."

Her English had that same inflection her mother had, but it sounded less formal coming from her. Another generation, another crop of idioms.

"Let me at least take your jacket. You'll be more comfortable that way."

"I'd rather not," I said. "Comfort is way down on my list of priorities."

Her gaze went to the bulge under my jacket. "I see," she said and her smile tightened. "Well, then let me offer you a drink."

She picked up a bell from a table and shook it a couple of times. Another maid in white appeared. There seemed to be a lot of little women in starched whites, scurrying all about. "Bring the Senor a…" She waited for me to finish her sentence.

"Let's talk first before the others get here," I said.

Her answer surprised me.

"What would you like to talk about?"

"Your father," I said.

"Oh, that."

"Yes, that."

"OK," she said with a shrug. She waved the maid away with the back of her hand. "Let's talk."

I looked into her eyes. Something there said she was playing with me.

"Who do you think took him?" I asked.

She fingered a lock of her hair, twisting and releasing it. "His enemies?" she said. The way she said it, the words sounded like they came from a California valley girl.

"Which enemies?"

She gave me a perverse grin. "How can I begin? Let me count the ways."

"Are you a fan of Elizabeth Barrett Browning?"

"Sure. I've read all her poems. 'How do I love thee?'"

"How many enemies did he have?" I asked.

She held up her hand, palm toward me. She touched the tip of each finger in turn. "Business. Political. Angry husbands. Angry fathers. He was a man of prodigious appetites. You are not talking about Little Lord Fauntleroy here."

"And you have no idea who did it?"

She shrugged. It wasn't a nice gesture.

"You don't care what happens to your father?"

"It's a matter of supreme indifference to me."

I waved my arm around the room. "Didn't he give you all of this?"

She offered me an amused look. "It depends on how you define the word 'give.'"

I wasn't in the mood for semantics. "Listen, Sugar. Don't play with me. Your father's been kidnapped by men who are very serious—he may be dead soon, if he's not dead already. I need some help from you instead of goddam word games."

You could cut her sarcasm with a buzz saw. "I didn't know you cared so much."

"You should be the one who…" I didn't get to finish the sentence. Three people came walking toward us, their reflections preceding them on the polished tiles.

Marta took a step backwards. "Shit," she said. "I have to get dressed. I can't stand around here half-naked chatting with you."

I didn't think she was half-naked. Maybe slightly underdressed, was all. She turned abruptly and said to me over her shoulder, "Introduce yourselves. I'll be back in a sec." That valley girl again.

I looked down the hallway. Jim Broadbent was in the lead, followed by a couple in their sixties. The woman was short, dark and appeared to be a Salvadoran. The man was European, big and fat, with a bulbous nose and a thick white walrus mustache. He had a flowing shock of white hair, parted down the middle. He was wearing a white embroidered guayabera, one of those shirts men in the tropics wear over their pants.

Broadbent grabbed my hand. "Hello, Hardcase. Where's the hostess?"

"Crying her eyes out," I said. "She's overcome with grief."

Broadbent wrapped his arm around my shoulder. "I guess I should've warned you about that bitch. This is a family that doesn't like to broadcast its emotions."

"Tough to prove it to me," I said.

Broadbent turned his attention to the couple next to him. "Allow me to present Ed Rogan. He is here from New York." He said to me, "Ed, this is Mr. and Mrs. Hoag. They're friends of long-standing."

I shook hands with them. Mrs. Hoag smiled pleasantly enough but didn't say a word. Mr. Hoag took my hand between his beefy paws and shook vigorously. "I am extremely pleased to meet you, Mr. Rogan." His accent was middle-European, from somewhere between the Rhone and the Danube. His voice was gravelly and breathless. Obviously a life-long smoker. "You are here to investigate the disappearance of Sr. Roderick?"

I looked at Broadbent. "The whole town knows why you're here, Ed," he said. "There are no secrets in San Salvador."

The room was very hot and I was starting to feel real thirsty. "I should've taken Marta up on that drink," I said.

Just like a genie, she appeared by my side with that damn bell again. This time she was wearing a full-length sleeveless black dress with a slit in the front that ran all the way up to her crotch. "Let me offer you that drink again," she said. She shook the bell and a maid appeared with a silver tray.

While the maid waited, Marta gave Broadbent a hug and kissed him on both cheeks, then she did the same with Mr. and Mrs. Hoag.

"What will you have to drink?" she asked Hoag in Spanish.

Hoag said, "Thank you. My wife will have white wine. I will have a double Johnny Walker Black with a cube of ice. No water." He pronounced the J in Johnny like a Y. Broadbent said he would have a gin and tonic and I took the same. The maid left and came back with the drinks and a couple of plates of appetizers. They looked like thick potato chips.

Marta led us to a sunken pit in the living room and we sat on sofas built into the sides of the pit. She took the plates of chips and passed them around. They were good but they had enough grease to lubricate your average sixteen-wheeler.

"What are these?" I asked.

"They are deep-fat-fried pig's intestines," Marta said, overemphasizing each artery-clogging syllable.

I kept on chewing. "You didn't see the latest press release on the federal nutritional guidelines, I guess."

Broadbent raised his glass and pointed it at Hoag. "Mr. Hoag used to be a partner of Roderick in some business ventures," Broadbent said to me. "They go back a long way together."

"Is that a fact? And when did you split up with Roderick?" I asked Hoag.

He looked up and to the right as he thought. "A long time ago," he said. "Perhaps fifteen years ago. We were partners for twenty years. Partners and friends…good friends." He looked at me without expression. "We were all very upset at his disappearance."

"Who do you think kidnapped him?" I asked.

Hoag laughed. It sounded more like a snort than a laugh. "The left did it, of course. The left have always been angry with people like us. We were not in the country during the war, so they could not get us. But they never forgot. The leftists have long memories. When we started to come back after the cease-fire, that is when they saw their opportunity. Senor Roderick is one of the great men of this country. To kidnap him is to wound the upper-class."

I looked at Broadbent to see how he was taking all this in. "What do you think, Jim?" I asked him.

He nodded, finished his drink and said, "It's a real possibility. It has all the hallmarks of the leftists. My only question is how did they get to the driver."

Hoag slapped his leg so loud his wife jumped a couple of inches in the air. She settled back in her seat with a sheepish look and sipped her white wine. "The usual way," Hoag said. "They threatened his family. They would kill his wife, his children…"

"Then why did the driver disappear?" I said.

Hoag raised his bushy eyebrows and looked at Broadbent and then at Marta. "That is interesting. I did not know he was missing. What has happened to him?"

Broadbent waved his hand in dismissal. "That may be important or not. People disappear and reappear all the time. People get drunk…"

Marta cut him off. "Why do you think it was the left? I do not agree. I think it was the military. Five million dollars is a lot of money, even for a fat ugly pig of a colonel."

Hoag let out a long low whistle. "Five million, Dios mio," he said.

"Keep it confidential," Broadbent said in an urgent whisper. "There's no use spreading around information like this."

Hoag nodded, then turned to Marta. "You always think the right is responsible for all the evil, my dear. That is your problem. When you do not have to fight for your money, when everything is given to you, then you believe the left is good."

Hoag turned back to talk to me. "You see, Senor Rogan, Marta believes the leftists are saints and the rightists are the devil. Needless to say, her father did not believe this."

Marta smiled coldly. "Unfortunately, I did not exploit the masses. You and your friends live grandly on the fruits of that exploitation." She reached over and patted Hoag on the arm, like a kid. "Senor Hoag and I have had many interesting conversations about this subject. As you can see, we have not been able to reach any agreement."

One of the maids walked into the room with some new guests. They were all the same types, mostly Europeans, women in couturier outfits with polished fingernails and high-rolling men with fat cigars and gold signet rings. The guests kept drifting in, couple by couple. Marta made small talk with all of them. Everybody smoked, so the conversation was punctuated by periodic hacking. Laughing and hacking. Hacking and laughing.

The dining room was huge, opulent and lavishly furnished in an old Spanish style. There were crossed swords, escutcheons and breastplates on the walls. It was like the medieval wing at the Met, only less crowded than on a Sunday afternoon.

Epictetus, the Roman philosopher, had written that it was unseemly to have more servants than guests at a banquet, but Marta had evidently not read her ancient Roman philosophers. When we sat down to dinner, there were twelve at the table. It looked like there were at least that many maids scurrying around the room.

Marta sat at the head of the table and I was on her right. She orchestrated the meal like Toscanini. The servants set down the dishes and picked them up at her direction with breathless efficiency. The main course was filet mignon. I knew from McInerny's little instructional lecture that the steak wasn't home-grown. There was a high probability that Marta had them flown in from Texas just for the evening.

Ah, the unadulterated privileges of being a Marxist.

The conversation during dinner was inconsequential. It was as if no one wanted to talk about Roderick's kidnapping. Or maybe it was just because I was a stranger in their midst.

After the meal we returned to the sala which had, mirabile dictu, been cleared of all plates and glasses and looked as pristine as when I first walked in. We washed down the dinner with rivers of Remy Martin and Courvoisier.

It was almost eleven. There wasn't any reason to stay longer. I got up and walked over to Marta. She was deep in conversation with Broadbent. She fell silent when she saw me.

"I want to talk to you tomorrow," I told her. "I'll call you in the morning."

She nodded wordlessly.

I shook Broadbent's hand. He leaned toward me and said into my ear, "Any luck?"

"Yeah. Wile E. Coyote did it."

I turned and walked down the long corridor to the front entrance. New guests kept arriving as if the eight o'clock invitation had no meaning in a world without rules.

Before I got to the door, Hoag stepped out of a hallway and grabbed my arm. "Senor Rogan, let me wish you goodbye," he said in his hoarse voice. He shook my hand and pumped my elbow with his left hand at the same time. Then he took a business card out of his pocket and handed it to me.

He lowered his voice. "Call me at my office. I have some information I think you will find interesting."

"Sure," I said. "You're going to let me in on the spiritual meaning of a full life."

He blinked. "Pardon?"

I slapped him on the back. "Forget it," I grinned. "I'll give you a call without fail."

CHAPTER 8

The parking lot of the Hotel El Salvador wasn't where you wanted to be at eleven-thirty at night. The place was lit by halogen lamps but the night was as black as the grave and there were large dark wooded areas on the fringes of the parking lot that could have hidden Rommel's tank corps.

Luis dropped me off at the hotel entrance. I told him to come back in half an hour.

The air was humid, warm and windless. It was quiet, if you didn't count the racket of the crickets and the noise of an occasional firecracker to signal the approaching New Year.

It was past eleven-thirty but Mayorga wasn't there yet. I walked around the lot with an uncomfortable twitch in the back of my neck, the result of many years of being in places I wasn't supposed to be, at times I wasn't supposed to be there. The hotel had some kind of function going on and men in tuxedos and women in long gowns kept drifting in and out of the lobby. As I swung around the outer edge of the blacktop, I came upon a couple engaged in sexual congress in the back seat of a late model four door black or dark blue BMW 728i. If they had that kind of money, they could've bought a small hotel. But, hell, lust and time being what it is…

They didn't see me, and I didn't want to break the rising and falling rhythm of the shocks, so I kept on walking.

Just as I rounded the far corner for the second time, and liking it less each lap around, a jeep raced into the lot and squealed to a stop ten feet in front of me. The driver didn't even have the common courtesy to lower his brights.

I walked around to the driver's side and looked in. The driver was wearing a uniform, but the man sitting on the passenger side was in mufti. The guy grabbed the windshield and hauled himself upright. He waited a couple of seconds watching me, then slowly climbed out. He said something to the driver I couldn't hear.

The driver gunned the engine, put it into gear and roared out of the lot as if he just remembered he had to take an overdue book back to the library.

Colonel Mayorga walked over to me with an easy swagger. He was a small wiry man, younger than I expected, with close-cropped curly black hair. He was clean-shaven and not bad-looking. He must have been in his late thirties, maybe five-eight. There was a kind of coiled tension in his walk. He was wearing a neatly-pressed white guayabera, a pair of tight jeans and well-polished cowboy boots.

He didn't give me his hand. He just stood there studying me. It was tough to see his eyes in the darkness, but I would've bet even money they were small and hard.

Suddenly he clicked his heels and inclined his head slightly, like a character in an old black and white movie. I almost laughed in his face.

"Mister Rogan," he said in English. "Jim Broadbent said I should give you a hand any way I can." His lisp made the words sound like the hiss of a snake. He should've spoken in Spanish. At least, in that language he would have sounded like the Captain from Castille, not some goddam gay caballero.

"How do you know Jim?" I asked him.

"We go back a long way." He waved his hand in dismissal. "What can I do for you?"

"You heard about Roderick?"

He grunted. "You think I'm blind and deef?"

"I want the scuttlebutt from inside the military."

"Who are you working for?" he said.

"The forces of enlightenment."

"Yeah. Well, let me give you some advice. You're here on a sucker's mission."

"Why do you say that?" I asked him.

He put his hands on his hips and leaned closer to me. "You got no idea what you're getting your ass into."

"Who grabbed Roderick?"

"I don't know, but I can nose around and get you the inside skinny."

His English was good, if highly accented.

"Where'd you learn English?" I said.

He broke into a big grin. His teeth were white and big, but he had too many of them.

"Man," he said. "I went to the Citadel and West Point. My little finger has more time in grade than your whole fuckin' body."

"What the hell do you know about me?"

"You? A jarhead." He laughed. "The Tet offensive in Hue. First battalion, Fifth Marines. Semper Fi and all that shit. I know all about you and your distinguished career."

"From Broadbent?"

He shrugged. "A saber. Who ever knows?"

"Who grabbed Roderick?" I asked again.

"You want my personal opinion?"

I looked deep into his shadowed eyes. "I want your professional opinion."

"The fuckin' guerillas. They need the cash for their cause."

"I thought the war was over."

"Wise up, Colonel," he snorted. "La lucha continua. The struggle continues. The rebels are broke. They can't get a peso from the

Chinks or the Russkies. Fidel's on his last legs. The Sandinistas are history. Where do you think they're going to get their dough?"

"What happens if they don't get their money?"

"They'll get it. Don't fret. Five million is cigarette money for Roderick."

"How do you know it's five million?"

He put his hand on my shoulder. "My friend, have you ever read *Alice in Wonderland*?" He gave me a smile that could have won points for sincerity. "Welcome to the land behind the looking glass. Everyone knows everything here. Everyone knows why you are here. And everyone knows you are on a fool's errand."

That made me feel real good.

CHAPTER 9

McInerny was leaning against the arm of a chair in the lobby, chomping on a cigar, when I got back to the Camino Real. It was almost midnight. He still hadn't shaved and his face had a ten-day beard. He'd been reading the International Herald Tribune. He tossed the paper on the chair when he saw me.

"I got something," he said.

"What? The clap?"

"No, I'm serious." He pointed his stogie at me and blew out a thick stream of blue smoke. "I got word Roderick's chauffeur was spotted in Santa Tecla. Want to take a ride out there?"

"Where the hell is Santa Tecla?"

"It's a suburb of the city," he said. "Fifteen, twenty minute ride from here."

"Sure," I said. I turned and started out the door. "Wait a second." I turned back to McInerny. "I told my driver to go home."

"No sweat," he said. "I have my ve-hic-al." He put the accent on the first syllable. "Follow me."

He walked out the front door and stopped next to an olive drab standard military issue jeep. The night air was sickly sweet from all the flowers in the hotel garden.

"Hop in," McInerny said. His breath reeked from a full day's worth of imbibing alcoholic beverages. I climbed in and watched him as he started the engine. "Well?" he said and he gave me a side-ways grin. "Do I get my story?" He let out his high-pitched laugh.

"I'm a man of my word. You got me information. Therefore you get your story. What do you want?"

He put the jeep in gear and took off with a lurch. "A rundown on the family Roderick?"

I shook my head. "Too broad. Ask specific questions."

"Who hired you?"

"Confidential," I said.

"Why did they bring down a ringer from New York?"

I hesitated, then thought, what the hell? The bad guys knew. Why not the press? It just might be able to shake loose some information.

"The ransom note was postmarked New York."

"Who was it sent to?"

"Guess," I said.

He didn't miss a beat. "The aggrieved spouse?"

"No comment."

His grin widened. We bounced over a pothole. I unholstered the Glock and checked the magazine. The safety was still on. I clicked it off.

He glanced over at the gun. "What's that for?" He drummed his fingers on the wheel in a staccato rhythm.

"My mother always told me to carry protection," I told him. I didn't know where this clown was taking me and whether he was on the level.

There wasn't another car on the road as we zoomed along. He was going way over whatever speed limit there was, if there was one. There was no moon and most of the street lights were out.

"Reach in the glove compartment," McInerny said.

"Why?"

"Hand me the camera."

I opened it and reached in. It was one of those old workhorse Nikons. An FTN, one kilo in weight.

"You going to take pictures in the dark?"

"There should be a flash unit in there too."

I rooted around. "Nothing in there."

"Shit," was his reply. "Feel around on the floor."

I reached under the seat. Imagine my surprise. There was a MAC 10 and the weight indicated it was fully loaded.

"Going to a birthday party?" I said.

He grimaced. "The natives are restless. I'm a peaceful guy normally, but peace has its limits."

I shoved the gun back under the seat. I was starting not to like the smell of this operation. "Where did you get your information?" I asked him.

"Tit for tat," he said, shaking his head. "Some things you can't say. Somethings I can't say. You know how G-2 is."

I grunted. "G-2 is usually wrong. I can tell you from bitter personal experience. Misinformation fed to the misguided who misinterpret it."

"That's what I like—a positive mental attitude." He jerked the wheel sharply to the right and we skidded around a corner with a loud shriek of protest from the tires. We drove past some shanties that were dark except for the telltale blue flicker of the TV set. It was the same old story. These people were so poor they lived in a shack with a dirt floor and no indoor plumbing, but somehow they could afford a TV. There was nobody out on the streets. They were all inside watching soap operas selling unattainable dreams.

We had just left the city when McInerny turned right and pulled into a middle-class street with postage stamp lawns. It was too dark to make out the street sign as we drove slowly past, but it looked something like Avila.

McInerny turned the jeep in a circle so it faced the house. All the lights in the house were out. It was a small, one-story structure. McInerny slammed on the brakes and jumped out. "C'mon" he said. He didn't bother to turn off the engine or the headlights. I did him the favor and reached over and shut them off. I wasn't going in like a schoolgirl on prom night.

The block was quiet. It was lit up by two lamps—one on each end of the street. McInerny walked up to the front door and rang the bell. I got out of the jeep and walked around behind it so I could see McInerny and the street at the same time. There was no answer to the bell, so he rang it again and then started banging on the door.

No one came to the door, so he motioned to me that he was going around back. I nodded to him. He was gone for a couple of minutes. Then he reappeared and shook his head.

"Nothing and nobody," he said.

He started walking back toward me when he tripped and went sprawling headfirst. "Shit," he cursed.

That was when the first slug hit the windshield. The glass didn't shatter. It just cracked into a spiderweb pattern.

Two more shots followed quickly. I hit the ground and rolled over next to McInerny. "A fine mess you've gotten us into, Ollie," I said.

He didn't answer. A trickle of blood ran down his cheek. I reached over and felt his temple. There was no pulse.

He was dead. Nice shooting or a lucky shot?

There were half a dozen more shots and then a couple of quick bursts from an automatic weapon, only this time they weren't coming from the far corner. They were coming from the corner we just turned. We were taking enfilading fire from both ends of the street. There was no cover. I was lying on an open lawn like a sheep waiting to be sheared.

I pulled out my piece and waited for the flash and fired a couple of rounds into it. That shut them up for a minute. The streetlight was maybe thirty meters away. I propped myself up on my elbow on the grass and squeezed off a shot. The light went out with a little crash.

The street was half dark now. This would give me half a chance to figure out some way to get the hell out of this place. Then some asshole at the far end turned on a searchlight that looked like it was mounted on a vehicle. The beam sent long shadows down the cobblestone street.

I rolled over a couple of times and sighted down the barrel. The searchlight was going to be tougher than a potshot at the streetlight. The Glock pulled slightly to the right so I made the adjustment and squeezed one off. It missed, but I could tell it was close because it hit the vehicle and ricocheted into somebody who let out a short grunt. The sound was sweeter than Beethoven's Moonlight Sonata.

I made another correction and squeezed off another shot. This one took out the searchlight.

Now the street was almost dark but it wasn't quiet. The boys at both ends of the block were hollering back and forth about the maricon in the middle who was giving them such a bad time. That would've been me, I guess.

"Get up close and finish that son of a whore," one of them yelled.

"Puta," the other side yelled. "You get up close and do it."

It didn't sound like any one of these gentlemen wanted the honor. I stuck my head up a little and looked up and down the street in the hope of some form of relief. In New York, every house on the block would've been lit up like the Christmas tree in Rockefeller Center. But here, no one turned on a single light.

Too smart for that, the civilians were. They weren't going to get in the middle of this little difference of opinion.

There wasn't much time left. Sooner or later, one or both of these groups of lowlifes were going to come rolling up the block to greet me.

Only I wasn't going to be there to meet them.

I crawled back to the jeep on my gut. As quiet as I could make it, I pulled myself up into the driver's seat and slumped down. The key was in the ignition where I'd left it. The passenger side was closest to the far corner with the automatic weapon. But I wasn't going that way. Not on your life.

I fired a couple of rounds at that corner, turned on the ignition, made a fast U-turn going over the sidewalk on the other side of the street and over some poor sucker's lawn, knocking down something in my way, whatever the hell it was, and took off back the way we came, flooring it and pumping off rounds right and left as I went.

I kept as low as I could. So low I couldn't even see over the hood. I just knew I was in the middle of the street but I couldn't see anything on the road. The jeep took a couple of slugs in the door and another one somewhere in the front that made it cough. The speedometer said I was going forty-five, but it felt like I was crawling along at five miles an hour. The jeep hit a pothole and banged my knees up under the dash and I let out a curse.

Then I slammed into something that jarred my teeth and brought the jeep to a stop. I stuck my head up to see what it was.

It was an old Buick angled out into the street. The jeep had run into the side of the Buick and was jammed into it at a forty-five degree angle. A guy stuck his head up not five feet from me. His mouth was open wide and you could see he had a couple of gold front teeth.

While I sat there and wondered what this sonofabitch was going to do, he reached into the Buick and pulled out something that looked like a flare gun.

I didn't give him a chance to point it at me. I put a bullet into the bridge of his nose and gunned the jeep into reverse, pulled around the Buick going backwards, cleared it, shifted gear and headed forward around the corner back toward the city.

Someone got off a couple of shots at my back but they went wide and then I was clear.

I was shaking in a pretty bad way so I drove back slowly. There were no cars on the road. I stopped the jeep about what I figured was a half mile from the Camino Real and wiped my prints off the steering wheel and the doors and the MAC 10 as best I could and started to walk back to the hotel. It was a long walk. All the stars were out and it would've been a beautiful night except for the minor detail that at least two men were dead and I had no more information than when I landed here and the clock was ticking louder and louder for Roderick and his bad heart.

I went up to my room, climbed into the rack and slept until hell froze over. I didn't bother to shower.

CHAPTER 10

Hoag's office was located in a neighborhood of large houses on a palm tree-lined street in a section of town called Escalon. There was nothing to indicate it was a business rather than a private home except maybe for the two cretins standing in front with automatic weapons slung over their shoulders. Then again, a lot of the private homes had guards standing around.

Luis dropped me off in front of the house and shut off his engine. I walked up the path to the gate and spoke to the nearest guard.

"I'm here to see Senor Hoag."

"What is your name?"

I told him.

"Yes, Senor," he said. "Wait for me one moment."

He went inside while the second guard shifted his weapon to the other shoulder and eyed me up and down with an impassive look.

The first guy came out and motioned me to follow him into the house. He took me into the living room, pointed at a sofa and said to wait. The room wasn't much to look at. It was furnished in a style that was frozen in time, like one of those styles that people use to furnish their house when they first get married and then never change over the years. This one was Danish Modern out of the Fifties.

After a couple of minutes, Hoag came shuffling out of a side room. He grabbed my hand in his big bear paws and gave me a hearty handshake. His voice boomed in his middle-European accent, "I am so glad to see you, Mister Rogan."

He was wearing a light blue guayabera that didn't do much to hide his generous waist. Under the guayabera was a pair of neatly-pressed tan slacks. He had highly-polished Gucci loafers on his feet. He wasn't wearing any socks.

He draped his arm over my shoulder like a long-lost compadre and guided me outside onto a large patio and pointed to a glass table with a white wrought-iron base under the shade of a bougainvillea.

"Do you like coffee?" he asked. "Real coffee?" He ran his hand over his thick walrus moustache.

"What do you mean, real coffee?"

"I mean Arabic coffee—Turkish coffee, whatever you call it in North America."

"You mean where the spoon stands up in the cup?"

He laughed uproariously.

"It wasn't that funny," I said.

"I like you, Mister Rogan. You are a man of few words."

"Yeah, laconic. That's me."

He looked at me, started to say something, then changed his mind. He sat down at the table and bellowed, "Nina Rosita."

I pulled up a chair and sat down next to him. The weather was pleasant, the morning sun was blocked by the tree and there was a soft breeze. The patio floor was covered with leaves that hadn't been swept up yet. Not a bad day to be hunting a kidnapper while a victim slowly died.

A little wrinkled maid in a pale blue uniform came out carrying a small tray with a small pitcher and small cups. She poured a cup for Hoag and one for me. When Hoag picked up his cup with his bear paw, it looked like a thimble with a handle. He took a little sip and said, "Ahhh….Gracias, Nina Rosita."

Nina meant a young girl. This Nina Rosita was older than the hills.

I picked up my cup. The handle was so small I couldn't put my finger through it. I didn't like the idea of holding the handle between my thumb and forefinger like a prissy schoolmarm so I just wrapped my hand around the cup. I looked at the coffee. The stuff was so thick it looked like pudding.

Hoag leaned over to me and lowered his voice. "I want to help you find Senor Roderick. He was my friend. I have some information, but you have to give me your word you will not say where the information came from."

"How do I know your information is good?"

He frowned. "Because it came from a dying man."

"Go on." I took a gulp of the coffee. That was a mistake. It was bitter as hell. I coughed and then said, "What did this man tell you?"

He glanced around as if someone was hiding behind a tree. There wasn't anyone in sight. The garden was large and well-tended. Part of it was a fruit orchard. On the fruit trees there were little plastic bags covering each one of the fruits. I couldn't tell what kind of fruit trees they were because I couldn't see the fruit because of the little plastic bags.

Finally Hoag turned his gaze back to me. "Let me tell you a story." He leaned forward conspiratorially. "A long time ago, maybe thirty years ago, three men formed a partnership. They formed it for one purpose only, because if they had not done so, they would have destroyed each other."

He looked around once again and lowered his voice. "No one knew of the partnership. Its purpose was to monopolize the commercialization and export of an essential oil called Balsamo de Peru."

I watched his greedy eyes as he told his tale. You could just visualize the profits piling up behind those tiny black marbles. It put me in mind of Balzac's line: *Behind every great fortune is a great crime.*

"Are you familiar with this product?" he asked me.

I shook my head.

"It is a valuable ingredient in medicines and cosmetics and fragrances, and has been used for centuries."

"Why is it called Balsamo de Peru if it comes from here?"

He raised his eyebrows and smiled at me. "Ah, that is interesting and rather clever. You see, the Spaniards did not want the pirates on the seas to know the origin of this valuable oil so they gave it a false name—a fiction. Because, you see, this product comes from only one place in the world and from one kind of tree only. It does not come from Peru. It comes from a coastal area of El Salvador called Balsamar from trees which are hundreds of years old. And no one can plant such a tree because it would take a hundred years for the juice—how do you call it?—the sap to be suitable for processing."

He stopped and nodded to himself, as if he were remembering a forgotten time. "This is not a pretty tale, my friend. These three men were among the richest in the country and they were hungry men. They set a price to export the Balsamo, but one man was hungrier than the other two and he secretly sold his excess at lower prices. Senor Roderick found out about this and..." He hesitated and inspected his fingernails. His fingers were like knockwursts and the nails were manicured and covered with a clear polish. He must have seen a cuticle he didn't like because he started to worry it with his teeth.

A hunched-over peasant with a straw hat came out of nowhere and started to trim the garden with a machete. The man was fifty meters from us, but Hoag dismissed him with a wave of his hand and a shouted word, "Later." The gardener skittered away quickly like a mouse caught in a bright beam of light.

Hoag finished chewing on his nail and returned to his story. "Senor Roderick—Don Jaime, as we called him—was not pleased, so he had the man's factory set on fire. It burned down but there was a further problem. The man's child was playing near the tanks of honey and was badly burned. The child was blinded and crippled by the flames. In this country, one does not call the authorities when there is a crime. You take care of it yourself, or your friends take care of it. So this man swore he would repay Don Jaime for his evil deed."

"So you mean this man had Roderick kidnapped?" I said.

Hoag shook his head. "Things are never so simple, my friend." He paused and brushed his hand over his walrus mustache. "The grudge lasted for many years. About five years ago, the man died. On his deathbed, he made his brother swear to revenge him." Hoag stared at me. "The brother made an agreement with the devil. Two of his workers were brothers of a priest who was known to have a connection with the Left. The dead man's brother arranged with the priest to have the Left kidnap Don Jaime."

Hoag leaned back in his chair and finished off his coffee. "Thus was the blood feud settled."

"Hell of a story," I said. "And what's the name of the dead man's brother?"

A grim smile came to his face. "One does not betray one's friends so easily. For this information, I will ask of you a little favor."

So this was one of life's little tit-for-tat games. I gave him a sour grin. "And what would that be?"

"I would ask you to carry a little package for me."

He held up his hand before I could say a word. "It is not drugs or anything dangerous or criminal." He shrugged. "You are a man of the world. It is a little gift for my…girlfriend in Miami."

"What is it? A battery-powered dildo?" This guy didn't look like much of a Don Juan, what with his girth and his advanced years.

He didn't catch my meaning. A nuance of language, maybe.

"It's a little something of no significant value. Something that would appeal to a young woman. I would be very grateful if you could do this thing for me."

"I might be here a long time. Your girlfriend might get impatient. I've heard women sometimes get impatient."

He shook his head. "You will not be here long." He gave me a knowing look. "Your work will be finished shortly."

CHAPTER 11

"What in God's name are you, old buddy? Some kind of walking disaster area?" Broadbent said. "I got a call from the policia that there was a rootin' tootin' shootout in Santa Tecla and an American reporter was killed. There's all kind of hell to pay. We have to write an official report." He squinted at me. "You know anything about this?"

Broadbent was waiting for me at the front desk when I got back to the hotel. The air conditioning wasn't working very well because he was using a big red handkerchief to wipe the sweat off the top of his shaved head.

"Don't even ask," I said. "You wouldn't believe me if I told you."

"I've been trying to reach you. Where the hell were you?"

"Checking out the local walruses. They get mighty uncomfortable in this climate."

He rolled his eyes and clapped his hand on my shoulder. "Come with me. Colonel Mayorga has something for you."

We got into the back of the embassy car and Broadbent told the driver where to go. We didn't say much as we rode along. I thought about McInerny. How much had he known? Had he set me up or was he an innocent lamb led to the slaughter? I'd always had an instinctive distrust of newsmen and McInerny was no exception.

Why was he carrying a loaded automatic? If I dug deep enough, I was bound to root out some maggots.

The colonel was sitting at a corner table with his back to the wall when we walked into the restaurant. He was wearing a dark suit, a black tie and a white shirt. He had on dark sunglasses so you couldn't see his eyes. There was no sign of recognition from him when we sat down. Impassive as a stone wall.

The restaurant was called El Bodegon. The decor was mock Spanish, like Charlton Heston in *El Cid*. The place was comfortable, quiet and almost empty. The air-conditioning was working overtime and the room was cool. Broadbent nodded to a man sitting with a young woman at a table on the other side of the room and then turned to me.

"Want a drink, Ed?"

"Last time I said no to that, I misunderstood the question."

"What's your poison?"

I ordered a scotch on the rocks and Broadbent had the same. Mayorga had aquavit.

"What's good here, Bobby?" Broadbent asked Mayorga.

"Have the camarones del rio," Mayorga said.

"They're crawfish," Broadbent said to me. "They're really tasty here."

"They're not crawfish," said Mayorga. "They're shrimp."

"You're wrong," said Broadbent. "Shrimp are small. That's why they're called shrimp. These are big. They're like crawfish, crayfish, whatever the hell you call them."

"What the hell do you know?" Mayorga said. "You're a goddam gringo shitkicker from the south who doesn't know his sister from a pig to be porked." The angrier he got, the more pronounced his lisp became.

"You dumb fucking spic," Broadbent said. "You get a little education at a second-rate military school in the States and you think you're a fucking Cordon Bleu chef."

I cut in. "Gentlemen, I don't give a good goddam if it's a friggin' blowfish," I said. "Can we get down to business?"

They both looked at me and then at each other. Mayorga spread his hands palm down on the white tablecloth. "You know I don't have any contacts with the Left." If he weren't wearing those dark glasses, I would have sworn he gave me a wink. "But I can put you in touch with a professor of religion at the UCA who has certain contacts, if you get my drift."

"What's UCA?" I asked Broadbent.

"That's the university. Hotbed of Marxism."

"I thought Marxism was dead," I said.

He nodded. "Sure. And so is Christianity."

"Who is this professor?" I asked Mayorga.

"My brother-in-law."

Broadbent looked surprised. "Seems like Bobby's family plays both sides of the aisle."

"Yeah," I said. "The Red and the Black."

Mayorga raised his hands defensively. "Hey, wait a minute. He's my wife's brother. You know how these teachers are. He talks a good game but he's just a harmless intellectual."

"Not likely to blow up any buildings?" I said.

"No, no," Mayorga said, sweeping his hand across the table. "He sits in sidewalk cafes drinking aperitifs and bullshitting about Marxist theology."

"Could he plan a kidnapping?" I said.

Mayorga stopped talking and looked at me for a long time. Then he turned to Broadbent. "Our friend is a suspicious son of a bitch."

"That's my job," I said. "How do I know *you* didn't grab Roderick?"

Broadbent cut in. "Listen to Rogan. He's good. He'll find your wife's maternal grandmother in hell if he has to."

Mayorga nodded. His mouth tightened. "OK, he might be able to plot something or other, but he's not the one to get his hands dirty, if you catch what I mean." He was about to say something when the man who Broadbent had nodded to when we walked into the restaurant came over to our table.

"Mister Lightener," Broadbent said and half rose to greet him. "Sit down and join us." He pushed out a chair for the man to sit down.

The man shook his head, then jerked his thumb back toward the girl he was sitting with. "My friend will get mad if I ignore her and then I won't get laid tonight. First priorities, you know."

He was an American, well-dressed in a dark business suit. His hair was black, cut short and neatly-combed. He had a thick dark mustache that suited his face. His skin was smooth and unlined, even though he looked about fifty. He stood straight and stiff. Professional spook, I thought.

He looked at me. "I know who you are and why you're here."

"Sorry I can't say the same," I said.

"My name is Lightener and I'm here to help you."

"I'm grateful. Seems like everybody in this small country wants to help me."

Broadbent put his hand on my arm. "We appreciate your offer of help. Mister Rogan is going to take you up on it. The embassy and the American people appreciate your offer of help."

"Yeah," I said. "And the rest of the free world appreciates your offer of help."

Broadbent jabbed his elbow into my side. "Mister Rogan has a well-developed sense of humor, but unfortunately he thinks he's back in the States where it's more appreciated."

He shot a look at me that would have stopped a charging bull elephant in heat. "Mister Rogan will give you a call."

Lightener nodded crisply. "Thank you, Mister Broadbent." He inclined his head slightly. "Gentlemen," he said and made an abrupt about-face and walked back to his young lady.

Broadbent turned to me. "Asshole," he said.

"Yes?" I said.

"That guy could be very valuable to you. He's one of the richest and best-connected men in the country."

"What's his background?" I said. "Is he one of your co-religionists?"

Broadbent raised an eyebrow. "Interesting you should catch that. You still have a good eye. He was with the Agency for twenty years before he retired. Mostly administrative, back in Langley, although he did spend some time in the field. Remember Ortega and Comandante Zero in Nicaragua? Then he married a daughter of one of the fourteen families, took over the family business and made it even bigger than it was. He knows everybody of importance in El Salvador and Washington."

"What are the fourteen families?" I asked.

"Just the richest people in the country, that's all," Broadbent said.

I turned to Mayorga. "What do you make of Lightener?"

Mayorga made a face like he'd just smelled a three-day-old corpse. "He is one bad motherfucker. I wouldn't trust him with the family silver. But, hell, if he can help you…" He shrugged and let it drop.

I said to Broadbent. "OK, you brought me into the game. It's your call. How do I contact him?"

CHAPTER 12

The next day I put a small advertisement in *La Prensa Grafica* asking for information on Roderick's kidnapping. There were two phone numbers in the ad—one was Broadbent's private line at the American embassy and the other was my room at the Camino Real. Who knew what would turn up? The ad promised a generous reward which, given local standards, could be anything upward of twenty bucks American.

Then I had Luis drive me to the country club which wasn't in the country, but was in the upper-class Escalon section of town. It was called the Campestre. Marta had said she was going to be there all afternoon if I wanted to talk to her. She wasn't about to disrupt her daily schedule for something as trivial as the kidnapping of her father.

The day was even hotter than the previous ones had been. I reluctantly gave up the quaint custom of strangling myself with a tie and wore my white oxford Brooks Brothers shirt with the neck open. But I kept my suit jacket on with the piece under it, after what had happened last night. The only problem was I didn't pack a sports jacket on this trip so I felt like a goddam geek the way I was dressed.

Marta was just climbing out of the pool when I got there. Aphrodite rising from the foam. She was wearing a string bikini made out of some kind of shiny gold fabric that looked like it would take a long time to dry. There wasn't much fabric in those three small pieces, and the fabric was pretty flimsy, so the bikini couldn't have cost much.

Her body was taut. It looked the way a female body does when it plays tennis and swims laps and gets a massage every day. She must have had some augmentation from Dow, because Mother Nature doesn't hand out a pair like that to many girls. Poor corporation, I thought. First, all those anti-war demonstrations for making napalm, then all those pesky lawsuits for breast implants. Seems you can never satisfy all the people.

Her skin was very pale, very smooth, considering that she spent a good deal of time following the sun. You could guess her migratory patterns. El Salvador in the winter, then Marbella in the spring and the Hamptons in the summer.

"Please hand me that towel, Mister Rogan," she said. She shook her head the way a puppy does.

I grabbed a towel from the back of a white metal chair and tossed it over to her. She caught it with one easy movement and started drying her body and her full head of red hair. Then she puffed her hair out with a brush from her bag. It was a vision of two metals. Her hair and her bathing suit. Copper and gold. Base and precious.

"You should put on a bathing suit and come into the pool," she said. "The water is very refreshing."

She was right. The sun was white hot and there wasn't a cloud in the sky. The water in the oversized pool was so clear you could see all the way to the bottom of the deep end. It was tempting.

"I'm working," I said.

She nodded. "Still, it is a shame you can't enjoy your trip."

There weren't many people around the pool. There were two couples at a table under a colored umbrella at the far side and some children in the shallow end. Their cries carried over to where we were standing. There was a fragrance that smelled like cotton candy in the air.

"Come over here," Marta said. "We can have a drink and talk."

She led me to a shady area under an awning next to the clubhouse and we started to sit down at a white table. Before we could get seated, a little man in a white suit carrying a tray walked up to us.

"Allow me to serve you," he said.

I turned to Marta. "What will you have?"

"A banana daiquiri," she said.

I must have made a face because she said, "It doesn't meet with your approval?"

"No, no. It's fine," I said. "Give me a beer."

"Si, senor," the waiter said. "Pilsener or Suprema?"

"Suprema, please."

"Very good, senor." He nodded and edged away from us without being so impolite as to turn his back to us.

I surveyed the pool area. "Nice Marxist environment," I said. "Too bad the proletariat can't enjoy it."

Marta looked around the country club, then back at me. She chose to ignore my comment. "Now that you have interrupted my swim, how can I be of assistance to you?"

"That's very cute," I said. "I wonder if you really care as little as you say you do."

She shrugged by way of an answer and said, "Do you have a cigarette?"

"I don't smoke," I said. "Anymore."

"Then would you please hand me my purse?"

I guessed she meant her handbag. I reached over and gave it to her. It was one of those Hermes bags, like her mother's, only larger. She reached in and rooted around for a minute and came up with a pack of Gaulois. She lit up with a gold Dunhill lighter and blew the smoke out slowly. Then she coughed.

"How many laps do you do?" I asked.

She smiled. "Fewer than I could do if I didn't smoke, if that is what you mean."

I looked into her eyes. "If you wanted to find your father, where would you start looking?"

She hesitated. I truly hoped she was thinking. Finally she said, "I really don't know."

She sounded like she was telling the truth. I tried another approach. "Who was the closest person to your father? Who was the person he confided in?"

Her mouth opened then closed. She took another drag from her cigarette. This time she didn't cough. "You should speak to his concubine."

I wasn't sure I heard her right. "What?"

"His concubine."

"I thought only Chinese emperors had concubines," I said.

She gave me a blank look. "You know, his mistress. How do you say it?"

"That's right. His mistress, his concubine. And who might she be?"

"Her name is Caridad," she said. She waved her hand in a gesture of dismissal. "She is a woman of no importance. Of no social standing. She simply managed to wiggle her female parts in front of my father and…you know how men are…."

"No, I don't. Tell me."

Her smile teased. "All men are like high school boys. No matter how old they are. They want one thing only. And they will do anything to get that one thing. Don't pretend to me that you don't know."

"Well, I've heard some men might feel that way from time to time. I think it has something to do with their diet."

She laughed out loud. "Mister Rogan, you are playing with me. I thought you were so serious. I thought nothing would stop you from finding my father."

"Who told you that?"

"Mister Broadbent."

"And what else did he tell you?" I said.

She stubbed out her cigarette with a quick jabbing movement. "He said I should cooperate with you. Although I don't know why I should."

"Why do you hate your father so much?"

The waiter came back with the drinks. She waited until he had served them and left. "My father never did anything for me. He never loved me or my mother. He was too selfish for his own desires. All he wanted was more money, more power and more women."

She took a sip of her banana daiquiri. She looked like a little lost girl sipping on a vanilla milk shake. She wasn't wearing make-up and her freckles showed against her clear complexion.

"Do you think the Leftists could have kidnapped him?"

Her eyes flashed. "All you capitalists think the Left are responsible for all the problems of the world. Why don't you look inside your own greedy hearts?"

There was no use getting into a discussion of dialectical materialism at this point. I was about to ask her about the concubine Caridad when a tall thin man in a very skimpy blue bathing suit walked over to us and slouched down in a chair without even being invited.

Very forward of him, I thought. "Why don't you join us?" I said.

"As you can see, I have already," he said.

"This is Antonio," Marta said.

"Your boyfriend?" I asked.

She giggled. "Heavens, no. Antonio is my brother." She corrected herself. "My half-brother."

"Of course you are." I felt like a jackass. I should've asked how many children Roderick had or, at least, Broadbent should've told me. The man looked terribly wasted, to put it as charitably as possible. Neurasthenic was a word they would've used to describe him in the nineteenth century. Nervous was probably the best twentieth century word. He was so frail he looked almost like a cadaver. His complexion was a sickly white. You could see the bones of his rib cage. His kinky reddish-brown hair was cut short and thinning. His face was unremarkable except for his long thin nose.

Marta started to explain the family relationship. "Antonio was the child of my father and his first wife. He is seven years older than me. We are very close, you see, because there are just the two of us."

"Are you a Marxist too?" I asked Antonio.

He shook his head. "Oh, good heavens, no. I'm a capitalist, unlike my sister. I work in the business with my father." His voice choked up. "I'm sorry. Please forgive me."

Marta gave him a dirty look. "He cares about our father. He's very upset about the disappearance of this great man."

"Please don't make fun," Antonio said. His voice cracked again. "He doesn't have his heart medicine. He may be very sick or even dead by now, thanks to your communist friends." He turned to me. "My father was good to me, very generous. He has given me many opportunities and many advancements in the company."

"It is not my communist friends who have kidnapped him," Marta said. "It is your fascist friends in the military who are greedy for our family's money."

"You are loco," Antonio said. "It is the Marxists that have no money who are hungry for it. They have killed many of our friends and classmates." He turned to me. "Many of our classmates are widows because of the Marxists."

"This is all very enlightening," I said. "But do you have any specific information that'll help me to find your father?"

Antonio shook his head. "I'm sorry. I wish I could help, but I know nothing more than the other members of our family." He started to cry. "I still think it was the Leftists."

"Stop crying like a child," Marta said. "You are a grown man."

"That has nothing to do with it. Men can cry also," Antonio said. "I am worried about him."

I put my hand on Antonio's shoulder. "Don't worry," I said. "I'll find your father."

I hoped he couldn't see the look in my eyes that said I felt as lost as he did.

CHAPTER 13

"The only reason I see you, Senor Rogan, is because my sister begged me to do so."

"That's mighty generous of you," I said.

The man seated across the table drinking a tall iced decaf latte was Mayorga's brother-in-law, the professor of theology. Evidently Marxist orthodoxy didn't forbid the imbibing of bourgeois beverages.

We were sitting in an outdoor cafe in the Zona Rosa section of San Benito. It was a rich neighborhood of boutiques and restaurants. I'd left Marta and Antonio about a half hour before. It was early evening and the sun was starting to set but it was as hot as ever and there was no breeze. Marta was right. I was sweating like a stuck pig.

"I'm here to investigate the kidnapping of Don Jaime Roderick," I said.

He frowned. "I know why you are here. It is obvious by your appearance. You are with the Central Intelligence Agency."

He looked just like a professor of theology. He had longish black hair and a full-face beard, all carefully trimmed. He was wearing a white short sleeve Lacoste shirt with the crocodile, that symbol of Leftist protest.

I shook my head. "You have it all wrong, Senor Lacayo. I'm a private investigator. I never worked for the CIA." That was technically true, although sometimes the truth has shadings of gray. I didn't feel like delving into the metaphysics of truth right now, so I let it go at that.

"You may make that claim, Senor Rogan, but according to information I have, you are here in an official capacity representing your government."

I shook my head. "Your information is wrong. I'm here as a private citizen, whatever you think of my government. Senora Roderick came to my office in New York to ask for my help."

Lacayo squinted at me. "Then what is your connection with the station chief, Mr. Broadbent?"

Needless to say, it made me kind of uncomfortable to know he had that information. The Left must have had a very good intelligence capability in the country.

"Broadbent is a personal friend of mine," I said. "We go back a long way. He asked me as a personal favor to help Senora Roderick."

I took a swallow of my coffee. Black, no sugar. "I don't know anything about a CIA connection," I lied. The coffee wasn't very good. It had a bitter aftertaste. Here was a country with coffee as its principal export and you couldn't get a decent cup to drink. I suspected it was probably because they exported all the best beans for the highest price.

Lacayo didn't say anything. He looked away from me and shifted his gaze out onto the street. I looked in the same direction. From where we sat, it didn't look very much like an underdeveloped country. The boulevard was broad and clean. The cars that went by were mostly luxury models, Mercedes and BMW. The pedestrians were middle class and well-dressed. Occasionally a peasant or two walked by. The evening was quiet.

"Let me ask you a question," I said. "What is Atlacatl?"

"A fiction, a myth," Lacayo said, without missing a beat. "There was never such a person. He was created in this century to give rise to false feelings of nationalism. According to the legend, he led his people in the struggle against the Spaniards which, of course, the natives of Cuscatlan lost."

"Cuscatlan?" I said.

"The ancient name for El Salvador."

"I see," I said, even though I didn't. It was becoming increasingly more and more difficult to get a clear picture. "What do you know about Roderick's kidnapping?" I asked him.

"Very little. Only what I read in the local newspapers. And I care very little also. Senor Roderick was an evil man. He was an exploiter of the people. This act is divine retribution for his foul deeds."

"Hardly divine," I said. "It's more like some sweaty crooks out to make a quick buck. The only question is whether these lowlifes are from the left or the right,"

He raised an eyebrow. It was the first display of emotion from him. "A plague on both your houses, eh?"

I shrugged. "It's immaterial to me who did it. My job is to find Roderick, and to find him alive." I took another swallow of coffee. "Who do you think took him?"

He sipped his iced latte, then unzipped his hand bag and pulled out a pack of Benson & Hedges. The bag was one of those small leather pouches with a wrist strap that Latin men sometimes carry. "Do you mind if I smoke?"

"Suit yourself," I said.

He lit up and took a deep puff. "Of course, I would have to say the military did it, but that is just from force of habit. I have a reflex response to automatically blame the rightists for everything. However, as I said, I have no specific information on the kidnapping itself."

I nodded. Maybe if I got him talking…"Tell me, what kind of theology do you teach?"

He looked hard at me. "I teach liberation theology."

"Is that a new religion?"

His look became colder. "You may joke, but it is one of the oldest religions. You may recall that Jesus preached against the ruling classes. I am simply updating Jesus' teachings and bringing them into the twentieth century."

"Does that updating include violence?"

"I am a non-violent man," he said. "However, in your case I might be tempted."

"Is that a try at humor?"

He shook his head. "I have no sense of humor. I am a theologian."

"I know some theologians who are pretty funny." I said.

"You are a cynical man, Senor Rogan. Perhaps in your country, theologians are funny. But here in Central America life is hard. I think you know Thomas Hobbes."

"Yeah," I said. "Nasty, short and brutish."

"Exactly. Your comments are too facile because your life has been too easy. Try to understand how the exploited masses live here under the most intolerable conditions while your friends enjoy a leisurely existence built on the toil of the workers."

"They're not my friends," I said.

"Then you are a fool because you are being exploited also."

"Yeah, that's me. Capitalist tool."

Lacayo looked at me. "Permit me to be frank, Senor Rogan. I don't like you and I don't believe you."

"I'm sorry you don't like me. I'm a lot of fun at a party. In addition, I'm an outstanding tango dancer, if you ever feel like going out."

Lacayo stood up. There was an expression of distaste on his face. "You are a fool," he repeated. "You will forgive me if I leave you to pay the bill."

CHAPTER 14

She didn't look like a concubine. A concubine was soft, yielding, compliant. She was fortyish, but on the hard side of forty. Her skin was good in spite of the deep worry lines around her mouth and eyes. There was a lot of black makeup on her eyes and she wore fake eyelashes. Her teeth and voice showed the effect of too many cigarettes.

She had been crying.

"You must save him," she sobbed. "My God, you must bring him back to me."

She didn't speak English, so I had to use my rough Spanish. "Do not worry, Dona Caridad. You can depend on me. Do not cry."

She nodded and tried to stop the tears. "Yes, Senor Rogan. I will stop crying." She dabbed at her eyes with a large handkerchief.

I waited until she composed herself. Meanwhile I checked out the boutique, trying not to look at all the female undergarments. There were a lot of different kinds of bras, panties, teddies or peignoirs, or whatever the hell you called them. I never knew there were so many varieties or brands. Olga, Bali, Maidenform, Playtex, Vanity Fair, Wonderbra. Evidently she worked the shop alone.

The boutique was just across the boulevard from the Camino Real, in a large modern indoor mall called Metro Centro. I'd had a breakfast of fried eggs with frijoles and salsa and tortillas by myself in the hotel dining room first thing in the morning and then walked across the street to her store.

It was kind of embarrassing to be standing in a boutique full of frilly feminine undergarments next to a woman who was bawling her eyes out while pedestrians strolled past the window and looked in at you. I hoped she'd finish crying soon.

Finally she stopped sobbing and looked up at me.

"Do you feel like talking now?" I asked her.

She nodded and rubbed her eyes again. "Yes. I am all right." There was a faint fragrance of perfume in the air that smelled good.

"Who do you think kidnapped him?" I asked.

"I know who took him. He spoke of it many times. He was always afraid that the guerrillas would come after him. He even dreamed of it many times."

"What do you mean?"

"He had bad dreams," she said. "Many times he would wake up in a sweat and could not breathe. He would curse them and then he would be bad to me. But I never stopped loving him."

"Was he bad to you often?"

"Yes. He was a son of a whore. But I still loved him." She started crying again.

"He was a son of a whore?"

"Yes. He hit me. He cursed me. Then he had sex with me. He was a very potent man. He was more potent than a man half his years."

"I understand," I said. "And why did he think the Left was after him?"

"Because he received many threats. He received threats by telephone and by mail."

"Did he show you these threats?" I asked.

"Sometimes. He did not want to talk about it. I think there were many he did not show me."

"What did these threats look like?"

"There were different ones. Some were written by hand. Some were written on a typewriter."

"Do you have any of these notes?"

"Once he made a copy for me because I begged him," she said. "This is all I have."

"Let me see it."

"I am not sure if I can locate it," she said. "I will try to find it."

She started flipping through some papers next to the cash register. It took her a couple of minutes, but finally she pulled out a crumpled sheet of paper. Her face showed a small smile. "Here it is," she said.

The paper was a xerox copy of a note written in a cramped hand. The writer had used uppercase and lowercase letters interchangeably. A grade school education, probably. It read something like this in translation:

Esteemed Senor Roderick,

For many years you have exploited the people who worked for you and profited unfairly from their labors. Now the people wish to reclaim the results of their work.

They feel that the wealth you have accumulated belongs to them. Please take care. You and your wealth are in great danger.

There was no signature.

I looked up at Caridad. She regarded me without expression. The note could have been either a warning or a threat. And it was reasonably polite—I mean, as far as threatening letters go. It was completely different from the one Mrs. Roderick had shown me in New York. That one was typed on a computer and it had a tone that was downright nasty.

"Were the other letters like this one?" I asked Caridad.

"Some of them were. Some others were completely different."

I was about to ask her another question when a customer walked into the store, so I turned around and made believe I was a brassiere inspector and attempted to blend inconspicuously into the background. But it's kind of hard for a big gringo in a dark suit to be inconspicuous in a lingerie shop.

The customer was obviously an American because her Spanish was halting and her pronunciation was atrocious. I walked over to a far corner of the store where I'd be less obvious. The woman said something about "push-up" and a "36C". I tried not to pay attention but it's hard if you're a man and you hear those dimensions being discussed.

Caridad came around from behind the counter and took the woman to a rack of bras. I didn't watch but I couldn't help seeing out of the corner of my eye because the store wasn't that big. They discussed something in low tones. It was a fairly lengthy conversation, considering the subject matter. The woman picked up a bra and inspected it, turning it back and forth and inside out. Then the woman put it back and chose a couple of bras that were hanging on a rack and walked to the back of the store and went into a little changing booth with a curtain over the front.

I wasn't thinking about "push-up" and "36C".

I started to walk back over to Caridad. There was something else I wanted to ask her about those ransom notes. But before I could reach her, I got a really bad feeling in my gut. Something small and black and ugly was pointing out from behind the curtain of the changing booth. I knew what it was.

"Get down!" I yelled at Caridad. I hit the deck at the same time.

The gun came out of the booth before she did. I couldn't see her face but I could imagine the look on it. "You bastard, Rogan," she screamed. "You son of a bitch."

She got off two shots in my direction before I could pull my gun. I was under the racks of panties. She was across two aisles behind a row of nightgowns. I fired a shot where I thought her gun hand would be. Her shots shattered the plate glass window behind me. A shower of glass came down on top of me. It felt like a bucket of needles falling all over my head and shoulders.

All the time Caridad was shrieking, "Oh, my God. Oh, my God," over and over.

The woman fired a couple more shots at me. But I'd rolled over and was under the garter belts. I don't know where her slugs went but I didn't hear them hit near me.

I shot twice at her legs where I could see them under the racks but she was moving and I missed her. I rolled over again. She took another couple of shots at me. One hit the bar over my head and ricocheted against the wall at the back of the shop. I fired two shots at her legs again.

Caridad was still screaming, "Oh my God. Oh my God."

The woman didn't wait around to be shot at again. From where I lay on the deck, I could see her feet moving toward the door. I pulled off another shot in her direction but, at the same time, she wheeled around and fired one at me. We missed each other.

Then she was out the door.

I holstered my gun, got to my feet and went over to Caridad. She was hysterical, but it looked like she was OK. I ran over to the door and looked out in both directions. People were screaming and running in all directions. There was no sign of the bitch.

It was useless to talk to Caridad now. I left the shop and walked around the mall looking for the woman but everybody stopped and stared at me. Then a man came up to me and said, "Senor, permit me to take you to the hospital."

"Why?" I said.

He led me to a floor-to-ceiling mirror. I looked like something that had crawled out of the grave on all fours. Blood was dripping down all over my face and neck. It was all those little glass splinters.

"Do not be worried," I said. "I look much worse than I feel."

❈   ❈   ❈

After they got me to the hospital and the doctors plucked all those little glass splinters out of my hide, I got Broadbent on his cell phone.

"Listen, buddy," I said. "Some wacko American broad just took a few potshots at me."

"And you think that's something out of the ordinary?"

"Very funny," I said.

"With your track record, it's a miracle more girls aren't doing that."

"Don't be a goddam comedian. I want you to find out who this broad is and why she's pissed off at me."

"Aye, aye, sir," he said. "And where did this alleged event occur?"

"In Metro Centro in the bra and girdle shop of Roderick's mistress."

He gave a short whistle. "Very interesting. And what did this shooter look like?"

"She must've been in her mid-thirties, medium-length light brown hair, with kind of a tight, pinched face.

She was maybe five-six, a hundred and thirty pounds. She was wearing a knee-length blue dress and shiny black high heel shoes. I think the gun was a Beretta. You know, one of those little jobs with the tip-up barrel. It sounded like a .22."

"I'll try to get a line on her," Broadbent said. "It's not every day an American girl goes around shooting up the place." He paused. "You OK?" he asked.

"Yeah, I'm OK. Just kind of look like a pincushion with bandages."

His voice became quieter. "You take care of yourself, now. You hear?"

"Yeah, I hear."

"I'll talk to you later."

"Oh, and there's one more thing," I said.

"What's that?"

"She's a 36C."

CHAPTER 15

It was a few minutes before noon when I got back to the Camino Real. There was a message from Mayorga that had come in at eleven o'clock saying to call him. I reached him at army headquarters. He told me he had some scuttlebutt and to sit tight. He arrived inside of twenty minutes.

He swaggered through the front door of the hotel in his starched uniform like he was the managing partner. He had on his trademark sunglasses. And this time he was wearing snakeskin cowboy boots.

"Hey, Colonel Jarhead," he said when he saw me. He gave me a sharp salute.

"Cut the crap," I said. "What do you have for me?"

"Hey, man. You should loosen up. You can't go around banging your head into everything you see. What the hell happened to you?"

"I forgot to duck," I said. "Now what's the news?"

Mayorga looked around. "We can't talk here. Follow me."

He took me to an alcove behind the front desk. There were a couple of sofas at a right angle with one of those chrome and glass coffee tables between them. He sat down and pulled an envelope from inside his neatly pressed shirt. He opened the envelope carefully and dropped it on the coffee table.

"Take a look," he said.

I sat and took the envelope. Inside was an eight by ten black and white glossy of a group of a dozen men in camouflage sitting around a campfire. One of the men was sitting on a rock while the others formed a semicircle in front of him. They all had rifles slung over their shoulders except for the guy on the rock.

"Notice anything unusual?" Mayorga said, pointing at the photo.

"What, no espresso machine?"

He shook his head. "Nah, the honcho on the rock."

I looked closer. The guy seemed to be smiling. "Why is this man smiling?" I said.

"He's not smiling. He's squinting," Mayorga lisped.

"He's squinting because he can't see?"

"Bingo, mi colonel. He can only make out light and dark. He's called El Ciego."

"The blind one?" I said.

"Exactly. He's the one you're looking for. He's the sonofabitch who kidnapped Roderick. Him and his motherfucking band of guerillas."

I eyed him. "How do you know this?"

"This came precisely from military intelligence." He smiled. "Our boys are good. They got people all over the interior infiltrated into these guerilla groups. The word is out on the street that Roderick is being held captured by an offshoot of the FMLN. One of their renegade brigades. They don't want to come in out of the cold and so they need to make a lot of dough to finance their operation."

"How do I get to talk to them?"

"You don't. When they want to reach you they will."

He got up. "You owe me one," he said and swaggered out of the lobby and into the midday sun.

It was time for lunch. It had been a morning and a half. I was so hungry I could've eaten the crotch off a rag doll. To paraphrase Winston Churchill, nothing stimulates the appetite like being shot at and missed. I walked over to the dining room but there was a sign next to the door saying it was closed for a private meeting of the Salvadoran-

American Chamber of Commerce. I was about to leave when Lightener walked through the lobby with two of his bodyguards and headed in the direction of the dining room. He stopped in front of me. This time he didn't have his little girlfriend with him.

"Mr. Rogan," he said. "What happened to you?"

I told him.

He shook his head and grimaced behind his thick mustache. "Jesus," he said. "Is no one safe anymore?" He motioned to his bodyguard. "Mr. Rogan, won't you join me for lunch? You'll be a guest at my table."

"Thanks but I'm not properly attired."

"Don't concern yourself," Lightener said. He turned to the bodyguard he had motioned to. "Armando," he said in Spanish, "please lend Mr. Rogan your necktie."

The guy pulled off his Joe six-pack tie. It was one of those polyester numbers with the striped gradations of colors going from light to dark.

It was my turn to grimace. "Not exactly my style," I said to Lightener.

He smiled. "I understand. I've tried to get Armando to subscribe to GQ, but it's not high on his list of priorities. And, obviously, I can't go to his house and dress him every morning."

I put on the tie. Lightener walked into the dining room. I walked in with him. His table was in the position of honor, right in front of the dais. He gave me the choice seat and sat down next to me. The two bodyguards took their posts by the entrance doors.

"I want my personal physician to take a look at you," Lightener said.

"I'm OK. They took good care of me at the hospital."

Lightener shook his head. "My doctor is one of the best in the country. He trained at Johns Hopkins. I'd feel a lot better if he examined you. Will you agree as a favor to me?"

I shrugged. "It's OK with me. But he has to do it today. I won't be in town tomorrow."

"Very well," he said. "I'll make the arrangements." He signaled to his bodyguards and they scurried over. He talked to them in a low voice that I couldn't hear. They nodded and the one called Armando left the room.

The waiters started to serve the lunch. There was soup and salad and something that vaguely resembled a member of the family of chicken as the main course. I was so far gone they could have served raw eel in aspic and I would have eaten it.

I didn't recognize any of the men on the dais until Broadbent walked in and took his seat in the middle. When he saw me he nodded and raised his hand. I finished the meal in record time. I wouldn't have sworn the main course was actually chicken.

Then the speeches began. The topic of the luncheon was Trade and the Central American Common Market. Broadbent spoke about the assistance the United States had given the Central American countries in their search for export markets. Then one of the other speakers, who was a minister in the government, told about the great strides El Salvador had made in diversifying the export base from the traditional agricultural products. A third speaker went on about the need for liberalization of trade policies with other protectionist entities.

By this time, the effects of the meal and the monotone delivery of the speakers were starting to take their toll. I was nodding off to the cadences of international trade issues.

Before the third speech was halfway done, I was dozing as peacefully as a baby suckling at its mother's teat.

CHAPTER 16

The wire fence was ten feet high and electrified. There was a roll of razor ribbon on top. The factory was a one-story structure the size of a square city block. Next to it stood a small administration building connected to the factory by a covered walkway. There were about fifteen uniformed guards in sight, all toting smooth-skin grenades hanging from shoulder straps and carrying M203s, which I hadn't seen since those days in that pluperfect hell so long ago. The M203s were standard issue in Viet Nam, a combination M16 and 40mm grenade launcher.

The factory was an hour's drive from San Salvador in a rugged part of the country called Santa Ana. The area was unpopulated except for a few shantytowns with dirt roads and the usual bare-ass kids playing around tin roof shacks. The few peasants we saw by the side of the road just stopped and stared at us as we drove by. There wasn't much work for them to do and little to interest them, by the expressions on their faces.

The countryside was thick with tropical vegetation, but it was turning brown from the lack of rainfall. The dirt roads were rutted and tough on Luis's old Toyota. My head kept banging against the roof as we bounced up and down on the worn shocks.

At the entrance to the compound was a blockhouse. Luis drove me up to the gate. I told him I wouldn't be long and to wait there for me. "At your orders, Senor," he said. He shut off the engine, leaned back in his seat and shut his eyes.

Three clowns, two in uniforms and one in plain clothes, took me into an anteroom and patted me down. They pulled the Glock out of my shoulder holster and admired its sculptured beauty with grunts of satisfaction. One of them mumbled something about giving it back to me later.

"Despues, Senor," he said, with a wicked smirk and a wink at his compadre. They took me down a long corridor and across the factory floor where antique machines were stamping out slugs for machetes and other hack and slice tools.

Most of the workers had bandanas around their foreheads, dirty pants, no shirts and no shoes. The racket was infernal and the place reeked with an unholy stench. It was hot beyond any heat I'd ever experienced. The vapors hanging in the air burned my eyes. It was a fitting setting for one of Dante's rings of Hell. Both the EPA and OSHA would've had a field day here. No safety devices within ten miles of the place. Knee-deep in industrial waste. But they turned out one magnificent machete.

The executive suite was on a raised platform five feet off the floor in the far corner. It wasn't any more impressive than the rest of the place. It was made out of cheap plywood and looked like it was about to collapse. There was a large window cut out of one wall so that the boss could survey his workers on the factory floor like a tin god. I walked up the steps and shut the door behind me. There was some weak air-conditioning and so it was just a little cooler inside. Two of the guards waited at the foot of the steps.

"Mr. Rogan. It is good to see you." The man behind the desk came around and shook my hand. His grip was hard for a guy his age.

He handed me his business card. It read: Dieter Strassberg, Managing Director. The man was a curious mixture of French and German, probably from that bleeding piece of land that had changed hands so many times over the centuries. He looked to be in his sixties, but in pretty good shape. He was short, no more than five six with a hunched posture that came from age. There was a gray pallor to his face. His hair was gray and thinning and he wore it combed straight back. He had large square wire-rimmed glasses. He was wearing an open neck light blue shirt and gray slacks.

He smiled. It was a smile that took some effort. He went back behind his desk and dropped into his chair. "Have a seat," he said. "Would you care for a smoke?" His accent was thick, but it had hints of Spanish around the edges.

I waved him off.

He leaned back and lit up a Viceroy, then tossed the pack on the desk. It wasn't much of a desk, just some planks supported by a couple of sawhorses. "You said on the telephone you had something to ask me?"

"Yeah, it's about Roderick."

Strassberg leaned forward and put his elbows on the planks. "It is really a pity. We were good friends. Everyone in our community is angry about it. Any one of us could be kidnapped. It could happen to me." His eyes became beady behind his large glasses. "Those bastards."

"Looks like your army here could hold off Attila the Hun."

He snorted. "These boys go to the highest bidder. I do not fool myself. Somebody offers them more money, they are gone." He spread his hands. "What can one do?"

"Pay more than anyone else."

He let out a loud guffaw. "You are correct. Plus acquire all the latest electronics and weaponry. This place is more secure than a military base. And my house is just as secure. The weak link is when one is in transit. Then you are exposed, even if you travel in caravan. Just like Don Jaime. He was careful as one could be, but that did not help him."

I looked at him. He seemed straightforward enough. "Who do you think took him?" I asked.

"The sonofabitch Reds, of course."

"I read in *The New York Times* that the war was over. The *Times* never lies."

He gave me a grim smile. "Shit. The war will not be over until the last communist is dead. It is like an anthill. You kill some, but there are always some more underground. I would personally like to stomp them all into the ground if I could."

This guy was more rabid than Jesse Helms, but not half as charming.

"What about the story that your family was feuding with Roderick and that you swore an oath on your brother's deathbed to harm Roderick and his family?"

Strassberg stood up and wagged his index finger at me. "That is bullshit. Any person who told you that is full of bullshit. That rumor has been around this country for a long time and it is a false and malicious rumor. There is no truth to this."

"Then how did that rumor get started?"

"Malicious people talking bullshit," Strassberg said. His gray pallor took on a reddish hue.

"Where there's a corpse, there's a stink," I said. "There must have been some reason for a story like this to get started. Some basis in fact. A story like this doesn't just get made up out of thin air."

He walked around from behind the desk and pointed at the door. "Be so kind as to leave my factory." He had trouble keeping his hand steady.

I got up and stood in front of him. "Sure. Just as soon as you fill in some of the blanks."

He stared at me. His eyes were very small. "Mister, I am finished with you. Get out of my factory." He reached behind his desk and pressed a buzzer on the wall.

It wasn't long before the riot troops showed up. Seven of them in their boy scout uniforms. He pointed at me. "Take this son of a whore out of my sight."

They had M203s and I had a couple of empty fists. Uneven odds, wouldn't you say?

They grabbed me and started shoving me toward the door. I turned around and said to Strassberg, "This isn't the end."

"It is for you," he replied.

CHAPTER 17

The guards let go of me outside the front gate.

"My gun," I said.

They nodded and laughed through gold teeth at each other, like I'd said something really funny. It looked like a jeweler's convention with all that gold on display.

"Imagine this, senor," a guy with sergeant chevrons said to me. "Unfortunately the man who has your gun has already gone home for the day. Come back tomorrow. He should be here at that time."

There was no use arguing with these turkeys. I cursed them with expletives they would've had a hard time understanding and thought about the six hundred bucks I'd have to charge Mrs. Roderick under the sub-category of miscellaneous expenses and confiscated weapons. I turned and walked to where I'd left Luis.

He wasn't there.

I looked back at the guards. They were still watching me with self-satisfied smirks. Just waiting for me to say something.

"Where is my driver?"

They broke up and started laughing and guffawing and snickering. Then they pointed somewhere in the distance.

"Look, senor. He has already gone. He left sometime ago."

I walked back to where they were standing. "Do not tell me lies. My driver would not leave without me. Where did you take him?"

"Honest, Senor," the sergeant said. "We do not know where he is. He left sometime ago without saying anything. You can look for him. He went in that direction."

He tried to stifle a laugh as he pointed down the single lane dirt road we had come on. The road was clear as far as you could see, which wasn't far. It went for maybe a quarter mile and then twisted into a clump of straggly trees. Even from where we stood, the racket from the factory drowned out any sounds of the countryside.

I started back into the factory. The three men blocked my path. "I want to talk to Strassberg," I said.

They looked at each other and then back at me. The sergeant shook his head. "Senor Strassberg does not want to talk to you. He said to remove you from the factory because he does not want to see your face."

I tried to bull my way past the men but they formed a scrimmage line and wouldn't let me through. "My face is not so bad," I told them. "It is better than most."

Three more guards joined our little discussion group. One of the new guys flicked the safety on his M203 and fired a burst into the air as he approached.

That caught everybody's attention. We all stood where we were, looking stupid. I started into the factory again and this time they formed a circle around me.

"OK," I said. "I just want to urinate."

They didn't buy that either. The sergeant shook his head. "It is not permitted. You cannot go into the factory."

"Then where can I urinate?"

"You can urinate in the woods or in your pants."

"OK, then I want to use the telephone."

The sergeant shook his head again, more vigorously this time. "You cannot use the telephone. You must go now." He pointed vaguely somewhere in the distance. "There is a telephone three kilometers down the road in that direction."

"Thanks a lot, fuckface," I muttered in English. It looked like I was confronted with what is called an impasse.

I started down that long, lonely road, wishing I had a cellphone.

I walked for the better part of an hour without seeing anyone. There was a lot of time to think.

The goddam case didn't make any sense. All the ends were loose. There was no indication as to who had kidnapped Roderick, although I was leaning to the Left. From what I'd seen and heard, that looked like the odds-on possibility. Maybe it was the guerilla leader, El Ciego, that Mayorga had given me.

But it didn't look like too many people wanted Roderick back, from the affectionate words they had to say about him. I believed Mrs. Roderick and I believed Caridad, his mistress, but it was kind of hard to trust anyone else down here. Lacayo, the leftist professor, was as slimy as academics come and Mayorga was a posturing braggart of a military man.

I didn't like Hoag, but he'd given me a good opening to Strassberg, so now I'd have to deliver his token of love to his girlfriend. Lightener appeared to be a straight arrow, but those Agency types were always tough to figure out.

Strassberg was the one to keep an eye on. He was the first candidate I'd had the pleasure of speaking to who had a good enough reason to kidnap Roderick.

And all these damn people disappearing. In the States, people just didn't keep on vanishing with clockwork regularity the way they did here.

And what about McInerny? Was he a Judas goat or a schemer who got blown away by mistake? Was he supposed to be killed or was it me? Or neither of us? Were we two guys who walked into a set-up or were we supposed to walk into it?

Nothing was getting me any closer to Roderick and the little time left was running by real fast. The hard fact of life was that I had no idea what to do next.

And where the hell was Luis?

I kept on walking until I came to a hamlet set back thirty or forty meters from the dusty road. It wasn't much of a hamlet. There were only six shacks, more or less in a semicircle around a small clearing. You could see there was no electricity in the village.

The flashback hit me then and it almost stopped me in my tracks. All those decades back in time in less than a second. I was a boy when I walked into a village just like this one, wearing torn combat fatigues, badly wounded and dragging a gimpy leg. Exhausted, scared and in pain. A boy who didn't know jackshit. Only that he knew he had to do what was right.

There were three men in the clearing. Farmers, by the look of them. They wore straw cowboy hats and ragged work clothes. Each one had a machete. I walked up to them. They didn't seem surprised to see me. I would've been surprised to see me, a gringo wearing a navy blue Brooks Brothers suit, a white button-down shirt with no tie, an empty shoulder holster and black wing-tip shoes in the middle of this jungle.

I smiled at them. "Good morning," I said, only by now it was afternoon.

"Good morning," they responded in unison in a soft voice. They looked down at the ground. Nobody looked at me.

"Nice day," I said. I didn't want to frighten them by being too abrupt.

They nodded. "Yes, senor. It is a nice day."

"Is there a telephone in the village?"

They looked at each other. One man shook his head.

"No, senor. There is no telephone here." He seemed apologetic.

"How do you call someone on the telephone?" I asked him.

"We walk to the next village, senor."

"How far is the next village?"

"It is about eight kilometers, senor."

I nodded. "I understand."

I looked down and inspected the ground, just like them. It would've been hard to grow anything here. The ground was creased with deep dry cracks. There were a few blades of brown grass and a lot of rocks.

One of the men moved a pebble with the toe of his shoe.

"Is there a car or a truck around here?" As if it would have been too much to hope for some form of internal combustion transportation.

"No, senor," the same man said.

"How do you get your supplies and food?"

"The truck will come tomorrow."

"I understand," I said. I didn't say anything for a couple of minutes. They didn't say anything either. Nobody moved. We looked like some sort of tableau, a waxworks exhibit.

Finally, I said, "Do you have any ideas?"

"Concerning what?" the man asked.

I wanted to say, "About how to get back to the twentieth century." Instead I said, "About how to get back to San Salvador."

They shrugged, this time not in unison. The man said, "If you like, you can spend the night in my house. Then, tomorrow, when the truck arrives, you can go on the truck most of the way to San Salvador."

"That is very kind of you," I said. "Very generous. But I think I will start on the road today and hope for a ride."

The man nodded. "As you wish, senor."

I was going to ask for a drink of water, but then thought better of it. I knew what the water would be like. Brackish and lukewarm. It wouldn't be ice-cold kumquat-flavored Clearly Canadian with a twist. "Do you have a beer?" I asked.

One of the other men nodded. "One moment, senor," he said. He went into one of the huts and came back with a bottle of Pilsener.

"Many thanks," I said. I reached in my pocket and handed him a twenty colon note.

He shook his head. "No, senor. You are our guest."

I nodded. I understood their pride. Dirt poor, but with a code that went back centuries. "Thank you very much for your hospitality."

"It is nothing, senor."

I shook hands with all of them by way of farewell.

"Many thanks," I said. "Until we meet again."

"May you travel well," they said softly in unison.

I started down the road again. The beer was warmer than room temperature. But it was beer.

CHAPTER 18

I walked for another half hour without seeing a car or even a person. It was getting very hot. The sweat was pouring off me like a waterfall. The days when I was an eighteen year old shavetail were long gone. My feet hurt and my back hurt.

The road kept on narrowing. It was more rutted and more dusty the further I went. I was beginning to doubt that it headed anywhere. From time to time, you could hear a bird sing or some kind of animal move in the undergrowth. The vegetation was thick on both sides of the road. It was tough to see more than ten meters in either direction.

Then it became very quiet.

I smelled it before I heard it. It stunk to high heaven.

A truck came around a bend in the road behind me. It was an old wreck of a vehicle without a bumper or a grill.

The windshield was so dirty I couldn't see who was driving. It wasn't going that fast.

I turned around and stood in the middle of the road. I could have stuck out my thumb, but this was a less tentative way of asking for a ride and I was running out of patience.

The truck didn't slow down. I was reasonably sure it would stop, but I wasn't a hundred percent sure. The truck kept on coming. I could jump out of the way or I could stand my ground and get hit. It kept on coming. This was a serious game of chicken.

You could tell the truck didn't want to stop. It didn't slow down. It just kept on coming and then slammed on the brakes at the last possible second.

It stopped a foot in front of me. Then it started to bull its way past me. I stood there and let it push me back. They weren't going to get very far that way. The truck pushed me back about ten or fifteen meters. Then the driver must've gotten pissed off because he finally opened the door and climbed down and walked over to me.

"Are you crazy, man?" he said in Spanish. He was a short man with a withered left arm and a broken nose. "We have to deliver our cargo. Get out of the road and let us pass."

"I need a ride," I said.

"I am not a taxi."

"That is obvious. But I have been walking all morning without seeing a taxi."

"Then continue walking, man."

The guy was not being very solicitous about my welfare. "I would be willing to pay you well. Just drive me to a place where I can find a taxi or other means of transportation."

He shook his head. "I have no time and I have no space."

"I will ride in the back of the truck," I said. "I do not mind."

He shook his head again. "It is impossible. Find yourself another ride."

The guy was almost as much of a hardhead as me. I didn't know what else to say, so I didn't say anything. He must have thought he had convinced me because he climbed back into his seat and the truck started forward. The only problem was I was still in the middle of the road.

"Get out of my way, fool," he yelled.

I didn't answer him. I just stood there.

He started moving toward me but I stood there like Horatio at the bridge. He kept coming and I kept moving back slowly. I mean, I may have been stupid but I wasn't suicidal. Little by little we moved, like some kind of slow-motion Morris dance.

Finally he jumped down again. This time he was holding a machete and waving it in my direction. "Son of a whore, get out of my way."

He was a little guy. I could take the machete away from him. He took another step toward me. I was about to grab his arm when the other door of the truck opened and a girl in jeans and a white shirt climbed down and said, "Ernesto, wait."

He stepped back and turned to look at her. "Do not have fear, Sister Angela. I will take care of him."

The girl shook her head. "That is what I fear, Ernesto. Let me talk to him."

"Do not trouble yourself with this dog," the man said. "I will cut him and he will get out of our way."

"No, Ernesto," she said. "I do not want that. We will find a better way."

She walked over to me. She wasn't much taller than Ernesto. She was thin, built like a boy. Her hair was dark and cropped short, but her skin was light. She looked like she was in her early twenties. Her appearance was plain, by most standards, but there was an intensity in her eyes.

"Can we work this out without killing each other?" she said in English. She had a New England accent, probably Boston.

"You're American," I said, like an idiot.

"Sure," she said. "From Woostah, Mass." That was the way she pronounced it. "What do you want?"

"I need a lift. I've been walking all morning."

"Walking for pleasure or for exercise?"

"Neither. My driver went missing and I'm trying to get back to civilization."

Her eyes flashed. She obviously didn't like my answer. "This is civilization. These are decent hard-working people."

I shook my head. "That's not what I meant. I'm trying to get back to San Salvador."

"That's a long walk," she said with a straight face.

I smiled at her. She was one tough broad. "I didn't intend to walk all the way. I was hoping I could hitch a ride."

She shook her head. "Not with us. You'll have to try your luck with someone else."

"Why not with you? If you don't have any room up front, I'll be glad to ride in back."

"You wouldn't be glad to ride in back when you see our cargo."

"Is that what stinks so bad?" I said.

She grimaced. "It does smell very bad." Maybe she figured she could get rid of me this way. "You can take a look."

I followed her to the back of the truck. What I saw put a new color in my paint box. She was right. I wouldn't be glad to ride in back. The truck was a flatbed with slat sides to hold the cargo in place. The flatbed was piled two or three high with skinned carcasses of cows. The cows were as stiff as boards and the legs stuck straight out. Flies and other assorted brightly-colored tropical insects swarmed around like so many halos. The buzzing of the insects sounded like an approaching squadron of Piper Cubs. The midday sun shone brightly on this unholy scene. And the stench was overpowering.

I had to take a step back. "Lunch?" I said.

She shook her head. "We're delivering this meat to a town about fifteen kilometers from here. You can see there's no room for you. Why don't you just wait for another ride?"

I looked at her. "Why did he call you Sister Angela?"

"Because that's my name."

"Your name is Sister?"

She put her hands on her hips. "I'm a nun."

That surprised me. "You don't look like a nun. You look like a kid out on a joyride."

Her eyes narrowed. "That's not a compliment. I'm a serious person, not a kid. My work is serious. I help people who are in need."

"Then you can help me."

"I told you there's no room."

I smiled at her. Maybe that would work. "Aren't you a sister of mercy?"

She raised an eyebrow. "That's not my order."

She was as unyielding as a stone wall.

"Then it looks like we've reached what is called a Mexican stand-off."

"What do you mean?"

"You won't give me a ride and I won't let you pass."

Her eyes narrowed further. "We could ride over you."

I smiled at her again. That seemed to make her mad. "You could, but you won't."

She pointed her finger at my chest. "You're a stubborn man."

It was my turn to put my hands on my hips. "You're pretty stubborn yourself, Sister."

For the first time she stared at me like she had a major problem on her hands. She didn't say anything for a few minutes. Then she started looking all around as if she was searching for a solution. Finally she said, "What do we do now?"

"You can give me a lift or we can stand here all day."

"It's as simple as that?"

"The choice is yours," I said.

She took a deep breath. She was obviously in a hurry. I, on the other hand, could stand here until hell froze over or, at the very least, until I had to relieve myself. "OK," she said finally. "You can ride in the cab. But only until we get you to some transportation."

"Fair enough," I said. "Your chariot awaits."

She gave me a dirty look.

CHAPTER 19

Sister Angela didn't talk much. A nun of few words. She was squeezed between Ernesto and me on the bench seat. Every time we hit a rut in the road, we bumped against each other. The seat had springs sticking out of it and it wasn't much fun getting stabbed in the butt at irregular intervals.

We drove for about twenty minutes without saying anything. I thought about the Food and Drug Administration and what they would have to say about our fetid cargo. Then I wondered if the meat was USDA Prime inspected. Finally, my thoughts turned to that warm beer and about how another warm one wouldn't be so bad when a red light started flickering on the dash. Ernesto hit the offending light with the back of his hand a couple of times, but that didn't seem to help, so he stopped the truck and climbed out. Sister Angela frowned. "What is it, Ernesto?" she said.

Ernesto looked up from under the hood. "It is the water hose. It is broken. The engine is overheated."

"What do we do?" she said.

Ernesto came back to the cab. "I think it is best if I walk to the village. I will bring back a new hose and some water." Ernesto pointed at me. "Will you be safe here with this dog?"

She waved her hand as if she didn't have a care. "Do not worry about me. I will be safe. But come back quickly."

He inclined his head slightly. "Yes, Sister. I will drive back here with Diego in his truck."

"Very well, Ernesto," she said. "May you travel well."

Ernesto started down the road and disappeared from sight.

I climbed down from the truck. "Care for a game of Parchesi?" I said.

"You're very funny," she said. "But I'm not amused."

"Do nuns have a sense of humor?" I asked her.

She climbed down and stood facing me. "Do me a favor," she said. "Let's not have any of these nun generalizations."

I shrugged. "OK, as long as you tell me why you don't believe in refrigeration."

She rolled her eyes. "Because that's the way they do it here, all right? Now stop asking me questions."

"Suit yourself," I said. "We don't have to talk. We can just stand here in the sun and contemplate the ways of the world."

"Fine," she said and climbed back up into the cab.

I stood by the side of the road for a couple of minutes. Then I started to walk to the back of the truck. I could see her eyes following me in the rear view mirror. We were stopped next to a stand of tall palm trees. I walked over to the palm trees and looked up at the coconuts silhouetted against the sunlight and wondered if you could drink the milk.

As I headed back to the front of the truck, I saw something glint for a second under the carcasses. Shiny cows, were they? Not bloody likely. There was a tarpaulin under the carcasses. I reached over and grabbed the metal rings and lifted one edge. The stink was enough to knock me back on my heels.

It wasn't an arsenal, but it came pretty damn close. There was a real smorgasbord of firearms from Uzis to AK47s to MAC 10s to M-16s. I went to the other side of the truck and lifted the tarp there. Some of the pieces looked new and others looked pretty beat up.

Some of the pieces were wrapped in waterproof covering, some were slathered with grease and some were left exposed.

I was still inspecting our cargo when Sister Angela walked up slowly behind me. She looked scared. The color had drained out of her face.

"Planning to shoot some more cows?" I said.

She shook her head but didn't say anything. She knew the consequences. Nuns had been raped and killed for less.

She looked up at me. Her eyes weren't half as defiant as they were before.

"What are you going to do?" she said in a soft voice. She sounded like a little girl who'd been caught with her hand in the cookie jar. But before I started to feel too sorry for her I thought about the people who'd buy the farm because of these weapons. Maybe most of them wouldn't be lily white and innocent of any crimes, but some of them would be, given the nature of fratricidal war.

"That was exactly the question I was going to ask you, sister." She knew I was addressing her with a lower-case "s." Her gaze went down to the ground.

"We were going to deliver this to the people of the village," she said.

I shook my head. "The people of the village don't use weapons like this."

"You're right," she said. "This is for the brothers and the husbands and the sons of the people in the village."

"You're out of your mind to get mixed up in this," I told her. "You're an American. This is a local matter. You should be tending to people's souls."

The spark returned to her eyes. "Not as long as they're suffering. My work is to make sure the people triumph."

So young and idealistic. "You're on the losing end, Angela. You're going up against unlimited resources in a battle that's already over."

She shook her head. "It won't be over until there's justice for the people."

"There's not going to be justice for the people for another hundred years, if ever," I said. "Give it up. You're not going to get out of this with all your organs in the proper place. These boys play hardball with cleats. You don't know the kind of bastards you're dealing with."

She stuck out her jaw. "That's my business," she said. "I know what I have to do."

Obviously the Dutch Uncle lecture wasn't having much effect. She was one tough little number.

She squinted up at me. "You didn't answer my question," she said.

"What question?"

"What are you going to do?"

I gave her a noncommittal shrug. "I'm not going to turn you in. This isn't my fight. I frankly couldn't give a damn what you do. I have one job here and it doesn't have anything to do with you."

She let out a long slow sigh.

I studied her very closely. "On second thought, maybe it does."

She caught her breath. Her mouth opened. "What…"

"I want a favor from you. I'm here to find a man who was kidnapped. A man by the name of Jaime Roderick. Do you know the name?"

The slightest glimmer passed across her face. "I've heard what happened. It served him right."

"We're not here to make political judgments, remember?" I looked into her eyes. "My job is to get Roderick back alive."

She studied me with disbelief. "What are you anyway?"

"I'm a private detective."

"You mean like Sherlock Holmes."

"That's right. He was my father."

For the first time, she cracked a small smile. "I've never met a detective before. Aren't you supposed to talk out of the side of your mouth."

"Yeah, well, I did, but then I had corrective surgery."

Her smile broadened slightly. "What's your name?" she said.

"Rogan."

"Mister Rogan," she said. "What kind of favor do you want from me?"

"I want you to ask around your old boy network of pinkos and find me a guy with the nom de guerre of El Ciego."

"That's not a nom de guerre," she blurted out. "He *is* blind." She was worse than a feather merchant when it came to keeping information to herself. You could see she'd come apart like a cheap suit under torture.

"I know that. I was told he has information on Roderick's whereabouts."

The truck gave off some puffs of smoke and a cough that sounded like a death rattle. Then it gave off a hiss and was silent.

She eyed me skeptically. "I don't believe that," she said. "The Left doesn't take foreigners for money. It's your friends in the military that you should investigate."

"You're naive, sister. I'll bet you a Glock against your Habit that the guerrillas have Roderick."

"What's a Glock?" she said.

"Never mind," I said. "Give me your carnet."

She didn't protest. She reached into her front pants pocket and took out a small cloth bag with a drawstring. The cloth was that woven Guatemalan fabric with the little birds on it. She stuck her thumb and forefinger into the bag and handed me her identity card. The photo showed a shiny-faced girl under flat lighting. Her hair was longer and her skin was whiter. The mouth was a grim line. You couldn't tell if she was frightened or determined. The name read Angela Paolella. Her occupation was, in fact, Nun. She was twenty-one. She'd be twenty-two in another month. She was five-one and weighed a hundred and five pounds. A little slip of a girl, she was. Ready to take on all the injustice in this miserable world.

"Take my card," I said. I pulled out my wallet and wrote "Camino Real" and my room number on the back of my business card. "If I'm not there, get in touch with a man named Broadbent at the American embassy. He'll know where I am. Don't forget to call me."

"I won't," she said. Her look was indecipherable. "How could I?"

"Don't kid me, kid," I said. "I know who you are, where you are, and what you are."

CHAPTER 20

It was almost seven p.m. when I got to the Camino Real. It had taken me the better part of the day to make my way back to San Salvador. There was no news on Luis. I was worried about him. The sad truth was I didn't know if he had a family or where he lived. It made me feel rotten that I hadn't even asked him. Insensitive, was what the feminists would have called it.

There were four messages. One was from Broadbent, one was from Marta and two were in answer to the ad in La Prensa, looking for the reward.

I called Broadbent first. He was in his office at the Embassy. "Have you had dinner?" he asked.

I grunted. I hadn't eaten anything since the bacon and eggs at breakfast and I'd forgotten I was even hungry.

"Stay put," he said. "I'll swing by and pick you up. I have some interesting news for you."

"What about?"

"About that cunt who tried to wax you."

"Who is she?" I asked.

He chuckled. "Got your attention, didn't I?"

"Who is she?"

"Sit tight. I'll be there in fifteen minutes."

❊   ❊   ❊

Broadbent was true to his word. He showed up fifteen minutes later. That gave me time to wash up, comb my hair and change. I discarded my jacket because I didn't have a gun to cover up any more. So I put on a white Lacoste shirt and a pair of cotton khaki slacks. At least that way I looked more like a tourist.

"You look like shit," he said.

"Thanks," I said. "I feel a lot better."

We went into the hotel dining room and ordered a couple of beers. I asked for Heineken, because the meal was on the CIA's tab. I figured that, since it was used to buying six hundred dollar toilet seats, my government wouldn't mind springing for a premium imported beer.

"Who's the woman?" I asked.

He ran his hand over his shaved head. "You're never going to believe this one." He took a long slug of beer. "Remember that American reporter who got killed?"

"McInerny?" I said.

"That's the ticket. This babe is his wife. For some strange reason, she took it into her head that you killed her husband and she is hell-bent for revenge."

"Oh, Christ," I said. "Do I need this?" I took a swallow of beer. It was cold. Cold beer tastes much better than warm beer, especially when you drink it in an air-conditioned hotel dining room.

"The worst part of it is we don't know where the hell she is."

"What are you telling me?"

He finished his beer with a swallow and ordered another one. "On her immigration form she said she was staying at the Hotel El Salvador. But she never checked in there."

"You're the Man. Now you're saying you can't find her with all your contacts."

Broadbent frowned. "She's not staying at any of the hotels. She must be hiding out at a pension or a private house. We have to check out a lot of places. That's going to take time."

"And meanwhile, what am I supposed to do? Sleep with my eyes open?" I finished the Heineken and asked for another. "Will no one rid me of this meddlesome woman?"

He grunted. "I know how you feel. We're doing all we can as fast as we can. The police are looking for her and our boys are looking for her. But we have to keep a low profile. We can't make too much noise."

"That does a lot to put my mind at ease," I said. "Now I don't need a weapon."

He looked at my shirt. "So I noticed," he said. But he didn't ask me what happened to my gun. Instead he picked up the menu and started to inspect it. "You make any progress on Roderick?"

"Not much," I said.

He let it drop. "What do you want to eat?" he asked.

"Anything but beef," I said.

CHAPTER 21

It was noon the next day when I pulled up at Marta's front gate. Broadbent had asked Lightener to put a car and driver at my disposal since Luis still hadn't shown up. Broadbent promised he'd do whatever he could to locate Luis or his family. I felt I owed Luis that much.

Lightener's car was a big improvement over Luis's ancient Toyota. It was a late-model black bulletproof Mercedes with a suspension system that was specially designed not to ram my head into the roof of the car with every bump. Plus it was air-conditioned.

The same little maid in starched whites swung open the massive front door. She showed me down that long corridor past the tropical plants in the glassed-in atrium and seated me in the pit in the large living room. She brought me a Bloody Mary without being asked and then disappeared.

I looked around. The sun was bright through the large picture windows. You'd think you would see motes of dust in the shafts of light, but the place was immaculate.

The phone call with Marta the night before had been short.

"Mister Rogan, I would like to see you," she had said. "It could be a matter of some interest to you, as well. Please come at noon tomorrow."

I sat on the sofa and drank the Bloody Mary and wondered how a leftist girl like Marta could live in the middle of all this luxury and not see the dissonance. Did she really give a damn for the poor or was she just a Nieman-Marxist? Someone like Sister Angela put her neck on the line with her actions. Marta could recite the Marxist rhetoric but how far did her commitment go? Did she ever take any active steps to help the Marxist cause? Any steps that could have gotten her father kidnapped?

A door opened somewhere down the corridor. Marta walked into the room and came up to me. I stood up. She was wearing a white halter top with a bare midsection and a long white skirt. The whiteness of the fabric on her skin made her look even more tanned.

"I am glad you came," she said. She gave me her hand. Her skin was cool. "Perhaps you wonder why you are here."

"Yeah, I wonder why, now that you ask."

She reached down and found my fly and unzipped it. With a smooth motion, she slipped her hand onto my member and started to rub it up and down, up and down, up and down.

Her meaning was unmistakable.

"I have a hard and fast rule against having sex with a client," I said.

She smiled at me. Her eyes were half closed. "How hard is it?" she said. "Your rule, I mean."

"Pretty hard," I said.

Some ethnic group has an expression that says: When the prick stands, the mind stops. At that moment, I didn't remember exactly which ethnic group it was. And frankly, I didn't care much.

"Come to my room," she said.

I followed her along another corridor that ran parallel to the one I'd walked down. She opened a side door and we were in a room with stuffed animals on a large white bed.

Then she kissed me and we were off to the races.

The sex act itself didn't last long. There wasn't much passion. It was sort of like two professional athletes who knew the moves and the form and the allotted time. The rules were fairly standardized, even though one player was from the States and the other followed the European style. The match was well-balanced. We kept pace with each other pretty well.

We ended up with the good old in-out. The fit was snug and the friction was good. Before too many thrusts we exchanged those precious bodily fluids. The noise level wasn't much higher than normal. A few grunts, a couple of moans, a sigh.

As soon as the action was over, I began wondering how the hell I got into it and how quickly I could get the hell out.

Finally I said, "Why?"

She didn't look at me. She rolled over and reached for a pack of Gaulois on the night table and lit one. "Because you are tall, good-looking and strong, and I was…how do you say…randy?"

"That's how the English say it, but not too often."

I moved to the edge of the bed and was about to pull my pants on when there was a sharp rap on the door.

Without waiting for the benefit of a reply, the door opened. It was Antonio.

He looked at us with a glazed expression. His lips were quivering. "Your mother is on the phone from New York," he said to his sister. "She is saying she received another ransom letter from the kidnappers. She wants to know what to do." He started to cry.

"Tell her not to do anything," I said. "Tell her I'll see her in New York as soon as I can get there."

The next flight out was at three-thirty that afternoon. I went back to the hotel and started to pack. But I stopped and checked a little more closely when I saw that some of my things had been moved. Not much, but enough to show that somebody had been in the room and had taken a leisurely stroll through my stuff.

There wasn't anything worthwhile in the hotel room for a lowlife to find but it still wasn't a lot of fun to have someone poking around.

OK, so we had just been rutting like two warthogs in heat. The question now was whether I was the fucker or the fuckee.

My stock in trade was facts. Somebody did something bad, took something that didn't belong to him, killed somebody he shouldn't have killed. Emotions were another story. It was tough to figure out people's feelings. Like Marta. What made her want to screw me? And did her reason have anything at all to do with keeping me pleasantly occupied while some person made an unauthorized entry into my room?

Was this another one of life's little unanswered and unanswerable questions?

CHAPTER 22

The plane landed at Kennedy at nine thirty-seven p.m. I got my car out of long-term parking and drove to my place to shower and shave and change. I poked around in the back of the bedroom closet until I found the old Smith & Wesson .38 police special. It took a little more digging to locate the clip-on holster, all worn and cracked and mildewed.

Then I took a taxi to the Czarina's apartment. It was a little before midnight. And it was cold as hell.

She lived on Fifth and Eighty-second, across from the Metropolitan Museum. It was one of those buildings that looked like it was designed by Philip Johnson, or maybe it was actually designed by him. They all looked the same to me. Especially on a moonless night in the dead of winter, with dirty snow still piled up on the curb.

If the doorman was surprised to see me waltzing into his deserted lobby at that time of night he didn't show it. These guys had seen just about everything and then some.

"Mrs. Roderick," I said. "Fourteenth floor."

"She expecting you?"

"Everybody expects me."

"That a fact?" He went to his console and dialed her number. "What's your name?"

"Tell her it's Rogan."

He spoke into the phone and then jerked his head toward the back of the lobby. "Take the elevator on the right."

I nodded. "I want to ask you a question."

His eyebrows went up. "Yeah?"

"You see anything unusual around here the last week or two?"

"Unusual? Whadaya mean?"

"In other words, did you see anything unusual around here the last week or two?" It had been a long day and I was totally wasted. Besides it wasn't every day that I got laid.

"You mean, like unusual things happening or unusual people hanging around?"

"Yeah," I said. "Something like that."

He screwed up his face as he made an effort to think. He looked like an Irishman on the wagon. The Clydesdale wagon, that is. His eyes were pale blue and rheumy and his large nose was discolored with broken capillaries. After a minute he said, "You a cop?"

"Private," I said.

He nodded. "Can't say as I can really think of anything."

I gave him my card. "If you remember anything, give me a call. There's money in it for you."

His eyes brightened. "If you're working for Mrs. Roderick, you must be good."

"So?"

He leaned forward. "My brother thinks his wife is fucking around, you know what I mean?"

"You mean, like screwing around?"

"Yeah, that's it." He nodded twice. "He's been thinking of getting a private dick to follow her and see who she's been fucking."

"And?"

"Well, isn't that what you do? Shit like that?"

I was too tired to explain to him that I was a high-priced call girl with an expensive clientele, not some common back-alley whore with a raging case of the clap. I grunted. "Tell him to call me."

The elevator operator knew which floor. The button for fourteen was already lit. He let the door close and watched me out of the corner of his eye as the numbers flashed by. When we got to fourteen, he turned so his back was to the wall. I was going to ask him which way when I saw there was only one door.

I rang the bell. Nothing happened. I shot a look back at the elevator operator. He slid the elevator door shut and started back down. I waited another minute and then rang the bell again. There was some movement in the apartment and then she opened the door. She was wearing a long red wool bathrobe over her satin nightgown. Even in the middle of the night she looked elegant. Even though she had just woken up. Not a single strand of white hair on her head was out of place.

Her eyes were red-rimmed. It could have been from sleep, but I wanted to believe she'd been crying for her husband. Maybe I was a cynical sonofabitch, but somewhere in this sad world I wanted to believe there was a wife who cared what happened to her husband.

She tried to give me a little smile. "Please come in, Mister Rogan." She stepped aside as I entered. "Let me take your coat."

I took it off and gave it to her. She put it on one of those fabric-covered hangers with a scented pouch and hung it up in the hall closet, but not before she casually checked out the label. "May I offer you a drink?" she said.

I shrugged. "Why not?"

"What would you like?"

The chances that she had a beer were about as good as finding a real virgin in a cathouse. "Do you have Jack Daniels?"

"Who is he?"

I shook my head. "Never mind," I said. "He's dead. I'll have a scotch on the rocks."

"Very well. Please follow me."

The apartment was large. There were a lot of rooms and corridors I couldn't see. It looked like it was in the process of being renovated, because workmen's tools and painter's supplies were lying all around the place.

There were pillars framing the entrance to the living room. Doric, Ionic, Corinthian? One of those. The kind without the leaves on top. I couldn't remember which. She escorted me into the room and went over to a bar that was built into the wall. She opened a little refrigerator and dropped a couple of ice cubes into a short glass. Then she poured me a couple of fingers of Chivas Regal.

The scotch was good. I'd forgotten how good. I finished it too quickly and asked her for another one.

The room was furnished in a traditional style. Old European, Louis quatorze, that sort of thing. Very expensive, very tasteful. The antiques looked real, or at least like very good reproductions. Persian rugs and polished wood sideboards. And what looked to be a real Renoir and a real Degas on the walls.

"Show me the note," I said.

She nodded, disappeared for a minute and then returned.

Her eyes appeared uncertain, nothing at all like the self-possessed look she gave me when we first met. She handed me the note.

> PUT THE FIVE MILLION DOLLARS IN A BLUE DUFFEL BAG. DO NOT TELL THE AUTHORITIES. WE WILL CONTACT YOU IN A DAY. IF YOU DO NOT FOLLOW OUR INSTRUCTIONS WE WILL KILL YOUR HUSBAND.
>
> ATLACATL

Nice and neat. Not as nasty as the first note. It was cold and professional.

"How did you get this?" I asked her.

"Somebody gave it to the doorman."

"Which doorman?"

She stared at me. "The night doorman. The same one who announced you. Why do you ask? What does it matter?"

I shrugged. "I don't know. It might be important. Does the door-man remember who gave it to him?"

She spread her hands. "I did not think to ask him. Perhaps you can do that?"

"Yeah. Perhaps I can do that. When did you get this?" I waved the note at her.

"This morning. The day doorman usually gives the post to the elevator man who puts it on the little table outside my door."

"So you picked it up with the regular mail?"

"Yes." She closed her eyes and nodded.

"And that's when you called Antonio in San Salvador."

"That is when I called Marta."

"Right," I said. I examined her face. Did she know that twelve hours ago her daughter and I were busily engaged in making the beast with two backs?

I pushed the thought out of my mind. It wasn't helpful. Concentrate on the matter at hand.

"Do you have the cash?" I asked her.

"Yes," she said softly.

How long does it take somebody to pull together five million bucks of cash money? How tough is it to do? The federal money-laundering statutes made it a lot tougher these days. You could always get the bills from overseas. There were tons of greenbacks sloshing around in other countries if you knew who to contact and if you were willing to take a haircut.

"Do you have a blue duffel bag?"

"Yes." She shivered even though the apartment was overheated and she had on that heavy robe.

"What's the matter?" I said. That was the sensitive side of me, asking the question.

She didn't answer for a minute. "I am afraid," she said finally.

She was not the Ice Queen anymore. Just a scared old lady confronting the dregs of humanity. I felt sorry for her.

"Would you be so kind as to do me a favor, Mister Rogan?" she said, almost inaudibly.

"What?"

"Would you mind to spend the night here? They said they will contact me shortly and I do not want to be alone."

I nodded. "Sure, don't worry. I'll stay with you." This lady was paying me a princely sum and she deserved all the protection and peace of mind I could give her. Even if she weren't paying me a farthing I would've stayed with her.

"I am sorry I have no pajamas to offer you," she said.

Her words hit me like the flat side of a two-by-four.

"What about your husband's pajamas?"

She hesitated. A second, two seconds. "He...I..."

"Doesn't your husband keep a pair of pajamas here?"

"Sometimes he does."

"But sometimes he doesn't?"

She regained her composure. "I am sorry, but there are no pajamas."

Roderick was a man who owned a Renoir and a Degas, and he didn't keep a spare set of pajamas in his apartment? It didn't make sense. Unless he didn't spend any nights in his own apartment.

"You can sleep in the other bedroom," she said. "I have already made up the bed for you."

I gave her a grin. "You knew I'd say yes?"

She made an effort to return my smile. "I am a good judge of a man's character."

CHAPTER 23

The heart attack machine went off at five the next morning. That's when the phone rang. I was groggy but I managed to feel around and locate the phone in the dark. I picked it up and listened.

The man's voice was loud and guttural. He spoke in Spanish with a Salvadoran accent. "I am Atlacatl," the man said. "Do you want to see your husband alive?"

"Yes," Mrs. Roderick answered. Her voice sounded very small next to his.

"Do you have what I want?"

"Yes."

"Do you have a blue bag?" the man asked.

"Yes."

The phone was cordless. I got out of bed and went to the door of her bedroom. I opened it and walked in. There was a dim light on her night table. She was sitting up in bed. I walked over and stood next to her.

"Go to Grand Central terminal at exactly ten twenty-five tonight," the man said. "At ten thirty-five exactly, go to track thirty-two. Next to the start of track thirty-two, there is a garbage bin. Lift the top of the garbage bin and put the blue bag with the cash inside the garbage bin. Close the top of the garbage bin and go home. Do you understand?"

"Yes," she said softly.

"Do not try anything stupid or your husband will not come home."

Mrs. Roderick took a deep breath. "How do I know my husband is alive?"

There was a silence. Then the man said, "Your husband's heart medicine is almost gone. Do not make me angry or he will die."

The man hung up the phone.

She looked at me. I was standing there in her bedroom in my skivvies. She didn't seem to notice, or maybe she was too much of a lady.

"Can you do it?" I said.

She straightened her back. "If it is necessary, I can do it."

❦   ❦   ❦

The day went slowly. I called Broadbent in El Salvador and filled him in on what had happened. Then Mrs. Roderick got on the phone and talked to Broadbent for a while. I didn't listen in on the conversation but, from what I could make out, she seemed to take some comfort from talking to him.

I toyed with the idea of putting a mini-transmitter in the bag but decided not to do it. My first priority was getting Roderick back alive. If there was a hitch and they killed him, it wouldn't have been worth the risk.

Mrs. Roderick made me breakfast. Scrambled eggs and bacon, buttered toast and some really good Hero strawberry jam from Switzerland, and strong black coffee. She just had coffee with skim milk. I guess she wanted to keep me around a little longer.

Mid-morning I grabbed a cab back to my apartment. I hated to leave her but there were things to do. I showered, shaved and changed into a clean shirt and suit. Then I checked messages and mail and e-mail and didn't find anything unusual, which is to say I didn't find any major job offers or any invitations to the White House. A little after noon, I walked along Forty-ninth Street and then down Lex in the bitter cold to my office in what used to be called the Pan Am building and looked over the mail.

Nothing special there either. Just the usual bills and overdue notices. Unfortunately the creditors would have to wait, again.

I dropped down in my old chair, swiveled around and put my feet up on the window sill. The sky outside the office window looking north up Park Avenue was clear and blue and cloudless. There was some ice on the outside of the window.

One hell of a situation. Mrs. Roderick was about to drop a nice bundle of cash with no assurance her husband was even alive. I had no option but to help her do it. There was no indication who Atlacatl was, except that he was Salvadoran. And there was no way of knowing how many people were playing in this game.

I slammed my fist down on the desk. It wasn't productive but it was better than putting it through a window. What a lucky woman the Czarina was. Her husband who had a paramour was kidnapped, her daughter was a nympho and her stepson was a sniveling excuse for a man. Just your average happy dysfunctional family unit.

I stayed in the office working on odd projects to pass the time, but it was tough to keep my mind off the Roderick case. I got hungry about two and went downstairs to grab a beer and a pizza at Sbarro's.

It was mighty considerate of the kidnappers to pick a drop-off point that was just below my office. That way I wouldn't even have to commute to my job. After lunch, about a quarter to three, I went down to the appointed location and reconnoitered the area around track thirty-two. I looked into the dumpster. It was half-filled with your usual New York trash, including today's *Wall Street Journal*, a cashmere scarf and a paperback by Salman Rushdie. I walked to the end of the platform, checked out the entire area and then walked back again. There was nothing out of the ordinary.

At five-thirty when it got dark I took the elevator down the forty-eight floors to the lobby of the building that was now called Met Life but would always be the Pan Am building to me. In front of the giant curving marble staircases there was a group of cherubic carolers with shiny young faces standing behind stacks of Christmas presents singing the usual heart-warming standards.

I went down the escalator into Grand Central. It was right in the middle of the evening rush hour and the station was packed with people all bundled up and heading home to what they thought would be the relative safety of their caves. I was heading into a night of the hell knows what but nobody even looked at me.

Track seventeen was where the five fifty-eight left from. Only I wasn't taking a ride on the five fifty-eight. I walked to the front of the train with the regulars and then I kept on walking. Right to the end of the platform.

When you are born in New York and you live there most of your life, you get to know every passageway, every tunnel, every short-cut. It's all a question of survival. A split-second edge over the other guy is all you need.

At the end of the platform was the skeleton of an iron staircase. It wasn't well lit. I climbed three levels. Nobody had cleaned it in centuries. There were cigarette butts and candy wrappers and wads of chewing gum. Graffiti on the walls said something about "Yo momma." At the top landing there was a heavy steel door with a push bar. I shoved it open and stepped outside.

I was standing in the cold and dark on Forty-seventh Street about twenty meters east of Park Avenue. The building behind me was Two Seventy-seven Park Avenue. It used to be the headquarters of Chemical Bank before Chemical Bank disappeared into the maws of the larger and more voracious cross-town bank named after Mister Salmon P. Chase. I took a small piece of wood out of my pocket and wedged it into the bottom of the door so it couldn't lock. The sign on the door said:

METRO NORTH
EMERGENCY EXIT
FIRE EXIT No. 3.

There was no moon. It was one of those New York nights that feels like snow is coming before too long. There were a lot of cars moving slowly in the evening rush and a lot of impatient horns honking. The wind was cold in my face. I turned up the collar of my overcoat and walked along Forty-seventh, then up Third and turned right on Forty-ninth until I got to my building, halfway between Second and Third on the south side of the street.

I changed out of my suit and tie into a sweatshirt, jeans and sneakers and a dark zip-up jacket. The .38 in the clip-on holster went on my belt. I shoved a handful of rounds into the front right pocket of the jeans. My heart was starting to pound the way it did before those goddam night patrols down that meatgrinder called the A Shau valley.

Mrs. Roderick was waiting for me at her apartment. She was wearing a black wool dress and no jewelry. Her eyes shone with a fierce intensity. There was no makeup on her face but that made her classical features even more stark.

"Are you ready?" I asked her.

She nodded wordlessly.

It was only eight-twenty. We had another hour and a half to wait.

"Let me see the money," I said.

She went to the hall closet and rolled out a big blue bag on one of those wheel carts with the bungee cords hooked on.

I lifted the bag. It was really heavy. "Are you going to be able to handle this?" I asked her.

"Do not worry," she said. "I can do whatever is necessary to get my husband back."

I nodded. She was an impressive female. I unzipped the bag and checked inside. If I was going to be tracking five million bucks I wanted to be able to visualize it. There in a jumble of neat piles held together with rubber bands was the answer to a lot of people's fantasies. The ticket to a world free of petty worries and inconveniences.

She answered my unasked question. "Yes, it is the correct amount, Mister Rogan."

I looked up at her. "No sticky-fingered clerks taking samples?"

"It has been properly counted by a responsible authority."

I couldn't picture the Czarina dirtying her fingers counting this filthy lucre. How long did it take to count five million dollars, I wondered. I zipped up the bag and shoved it back toward her. "You don't happen to have a beer?" I said.

She wrinkled up her nose. "I detest beer."

"That's what I thought," I said. "I just wanted to make sure."

CHAPTER 24

At nine forty-five, the Czarina buzzed the night doorman on the intercom and told him to hail a cab. We rolled the blue bag into the elevator and rode down without a word. If the elevator man thought this was unusual, he didn't give a sign.

It was starting to snow. The flakes were coming down in heavy swirls and sticking to the sidewalk. The taxi was waiting for us at the curb. Our friend the doorman opened the door for us and gave me a wink as I passed him. He was probably thinking about his brother's wife giving pleasure to half of the guys in the neighborhood and maybe even considering getting a taste of it himself.

The taxi driver popped the trunk from the driver's seat. I went around to the back of the cab and slammed the trunk shut.

"We'll take the bag inside," I said to the driver. He shrugged and turned his head to face forward. "OK, boss," he said. "You are the boss." He was from the subcontinent, maybe India or Pakistan. He had a full-face bushy black beard and he wore a turban with all the hair tucked up inside.

The Czarina got into the cab first. I lifted the bag and put it on the floor between us. A strong odor of Chana Batura with a hint of curry hit me as we climbed into the cab. "Grand Central," I told the driver.

"Yes, boss," he said. "We go down Fifth Avenue, boss?"

"Go down Park," I said. "It'll be faster."

"Yes, boss. You know best."

We took off like the starting line at the Indy 500 when the flag goes down. The force slammed us back against the seat. Mrs. Roderick looked at me with eyes wide open.

"Take it easy, fella," I said. "We have plenty of time. No need to beat the clock."

"Sorry, boss. It is my way. Sometimes I forget."

I checked out his license on the dashboard. His name looked like a dish on the menu in a restaurant called Punjab. I was starting to get hungry.

The snow was coming down so hard the driver had to turn on his wipers. We drove down Park Avenue until we hit Fifty-fifth Street. I told the driver to pull over to the west side of Park and wait. He slowed down and double parked in front of the Racquet Club. The traffic going by wasn't so heavy at this time of night.

I turned toward her. Her face was white in the reflected light of the club lobby. She bit her lower lip. "Is this where you get out?" she said. She sounded like a little girl.

I nodded and reached over and put my hand square on top of hers. It was the first time I'd touched her. Her hand was cold.

"Are you sure you can do it?" I said. "If you want me to, I can do it for you."

She smiled bravely and put her hand on mine. "Thank you, Mister Rogan, but this is something I must do. Just as you will do exactly as you must. Each one of us has his own task."

She was dead right about that.

※   ※   ※

The cab pulled away from the curb and headed south on Park. The whiteness of her hair was visible through the rear window. I hoped she'd be able to hold up her end.

It was ten-fourteen. We were on schedule. I crossed Park Avenue and walked through the snow on the east side of the avenue, past the

Waldorf until I got to Forty-seventh. I made the left turn and walked the few steps to the fire door. It swung open without too much of an effort.

I stepped inside and looked around. There was an incandescent bulb in the ceiling that gave a little light. The door slammed behind me. I started down the staircase. Three flights and I was on the platform. There was no one in sight.

I jumped off the platform and started to the right over the tracks. The rats were surprised to see me. They were oversized and looked nasty, but they were decent enough to scurry out of my way without attacking an outsider who had invaded their territory. The main trick was to get from track seventeen to track thirty-two without frying myself on the third rails.

The only lights were widely-spaced incandescent bulbs. It was tough to move quickly over the gravel and the crossties. The shadows were treacherous because you couldn't see where you were stepping. There was the occasional rumble of a train moving and then the whole place started to vibrate. It smelled dank and musty like the grave.

I crossed track after track without falling. That in itself was an accomplishment. Track thirty-two was just ahead. But before I got there, I slipped in a puddle and went down on my elbows. I didn't move for a minute. Just looked around and surveyed the situation. It was quiet. No one around. I got up but stayed in a crouch and moved over to track thirty-two.

The only thing I was worried about right now was an incoming train. But then I told myself to forget about that. If these kidnappers were any good and had done their homework, there wouldn't be any incoming.

I was on time and in position. It was ten thirty-one. I was on the track at the end of the platform with a clear field of fire and a view of the dumpster and the entrance to the platform from the station. The lighting was fluorescent and a lot brighter than before. I stayed on the tracks and edged closer to the entrance, crouching below the level of the platform.

The butt of the gun jabbed into my ribcage. I pulled it out and held it in my right hand. Very slowly I moved closer. I raised my head a little and sighted down the platform.

Two men stood there. Their backs were toward me. They were watching the station. They weren't expecting anybody to come up behind them. One was just inside the entrance to the platform making believe he was talking on a pay phone. He was wearing a long dark overcoat with the collar turned up and a fedora pulled down over his eyes. The other guy was inside the station leaning against the gate. He was shorter than the first man. He wore a shearling coat and a navy blue knit cap. There was no one else around.

At ten thirty-five exactly, Mrs. Roderick appeared. Outstanding gal. She walked through the gate without looking at the men, pulling the cart behind her. She moved like a queen. Her head was held high and her back was straight. Carefully, regally, she stepped up to the dumpster. It looked like some kind of ritual disposal ceremony. She raised the top of the dumpster with some difficulty. Then she unhooked the bungee cords and picked up the blue bag. I could see she had trouble lifting the bag because she wedged it between her body and the side of the dumpster. She brought the bag up little by little until it reached the top. Then she gave a push and it fell into the dumpster. Most expensive garbage she ever tossed away. She reached up and slammed the cover down. It closed with a loud bang.

Not once did she flinch or make a misstep. Without a single unnecessary move, she turned sharply and strode out of view, taking the cart with her. I was really proud of her.

As soon as she was gone, the guy in the shearling stepped over to the dumpster, reached in and pulled the bag out. He nodded to the other man and they walked out into the station together, taking one last look around. They didn't see me.

It was lock and load time.

I pulled myself up onto the platform and went after them. I shoved the .38 back into the holster and zipped up the jacket as I ran. They were fifteen meters ahead of me. The shearling guy held the bag in his right hand and the fedora guy was on his right so the bag was between them.

They crossed the main waiting room, heading southeast toward Lexington Avenue. They moved at a good pace. The station was almost empty, except for the bums. It was too late for the commuters and too early for the theatergoers. The fedora guy had taps on his shoes and they made loud clicks on the stone floor.

I was twenty paces behind them, keeping my distance.

Shearling moved like the bag was heavy. He shifted the bag to his left hand. Fedora moved around to the other side so the bag stayed between them. They went down the southernmost passageway and exited out onto Lexington Avenue.

I followed them out of the station. Shearling climbed into the back seat of a dark Chevy that was double parked outside the entrance. He had the bag with him. There wasn't a cab in sight. I cursed under my breath. He slammed the door shut behind him and the car pulled into the flow of traffic. The car had New York plates. All I could catch was the last three figures-4MS. I was left standing there on the curb in a snowstorm while five million bucks drove away.

Fedora turned and walked south on Lex. There was no other option. I followed him.

CHAPTER 25

The snow covered the ground. It was a good thing I was wearing sneakers because I could move quickly. It was easy to keep pace with Fedora. He walked slowly and kept looking around behind him. He still hadn't seen me, as far as I could tell.

He walked down Lex past the Cuban mission and the Soldiers, Sailors and Airmen's Club and went east on Thirty-sixth. His collar was turned up and his hat was pulled down, and he walked hunched over against the wind. I hadn't been able to get a good look at his face. All I could tell was that he had a thick dark goatee.

He walked along Thirty-sixth past Sniffen Court with those upscale little houses until he got to Third Avenue and then he turned right. He kept on going south on Third. I was half a block behind him on the other side of the avenue.

We were getting into the region of the hookers, the pushers and the all-night cafeterias. The neighborhood kept deteriorating with each block we passed. Fedora kept on walking to Twenty-fourth. Then he turned right on Twenty-fourth and walked a few steps to a car that was parked a couple of car lengths from the corner. He bent down and looked into the car. From where I stood it looked like a Lincoln Town Car. It was dark colored, probably black.

There was a man in the car. I couldn't see what he looked like. Fedora walked around the front of the car to the driver's side and stood there talking to the man.

I stepped back into the doorway of a three-story building, glad to get out of the snow. My feet were wet and cold. I stamped them to get the circulation going. So far it had been a long and unproductive night.

A girl came wandering down the street and hesitated when she saw me. She eyed me up and down. Then she stepped into the doorway with me. She was about seventeen or eighteen. Her hair was ratty under a kerchief. She was shivering and her nose was running from the cold. She was badly strung out.

"Hey, Mister," she said in a loud voice. "You wanna have some fun?" She looked into my eyes. "I'll suck the veins right out of your balls."

It didn't sound very appetizing. "Ordinarily, I'd love to, honey, but I just got circumcised and that's the last thing on my mind right now."

She hadn't heard that one before. She blinked a couple of times to make sure she got it right.

I gave her a twenty. "Get yourself some hot soup," I said. I knew she wouldn't.

She shoved the bill into her coat pocket. "Thanks, Mister. You're a prince. When your circumcision gets better, next time I'll give you a blowjob on the house."

Which house was that, I wondered. The House of the Rising Sun? I smiled at her. "Thanks, honey. I'll save that one in my hope chest."

She turned and shuffled back the way she'd come. Either she wasn't going anywhere or she'd forgotten where she was heading.

I looked back to where the two men were talking. The snow made it tough to see very well. The street was quiet and there weren't any pedestrians. Most people were warm and dry indoors, except for those fools who chose to be outdoors in this foul weather.

The men continued talking for a few minutes. This wasn't very interesting. And it wasn't very helpful. I looked away and checked the surroundings. But when I looked back, the guy with the fedora had a gun out and was pointing it at the man in the car.

The smack of adrenaline hit me and woke me up. I yelled, "Hey, look out!"

It was too late. Fedora pumped out four shots, each one illuminated by a muzzle flash, then turned to look at me. Our eyes locked. For the first time I had a good look at his face. He fired one shot in my direction. I went back against the wall out of his line of fire. I pulled the .38 and got one off at him. He turned and ran.

I ducked low behind the parked cars and started after him. As I ran, I passed the car with the man in it and looked in. The driver's window was shattered and the guy was slumped back against the seat. His face was a bloody mess. I reached in and felt his carotid. My hand was shaking. I tried to steady it.

Nothing. He'd gone to his reward, whatever that was.

Fedora was halfway down the block on the other side. I stayed on my side of the street and ran in a crouch. As he rounded Lex he lost his balance and went down.

I was gasping for breath. The cold air hurt my lungs as I sucked it in. I stopped and put the .38 on the roof of a car and waited for him to get up and back into view. When he stood his head was bare. He'd lost the hat. He was standing in the flashing lights of a porno store. In that half-second before he started running again, I lined up the shot and squeezed.

The old stand-by Smith & Wesson was not half bad. I must have hit him in the left upper arm or shoulder because he jerked around with his right hand to grab his arm.

I went after him, staying low. I got to the corner of Lex and looked up the avenue. He wasn't there. He wasn't on this side or the other side of the avenue. He wasn't anywhere in sight.

His hat was on the ground. I picked it up. He must have been like Little Black Sambo, that character who just melted into the ground. I looked into the porno shop. There were a couple of guys in there, but not him.

I crossed Lex and looked up and down, keeping an eye on the door of the porno store. Still no luck. I put away the gun and crossed back to the other side of Lex and went into the store. Maybe he was in one of those little private viewing booths.

The man behind the counter didn't look directly at me. He looked at the hat in my hand. "Help you?" he said.

"You see a guy come in here holding his arm?" I said.

His gaze went to my face but he didn't look at my eyes. "Listen, you. No fags in here. You want fag business, you go to the next block. You get my drift?"

I shrugged. No use explaining to him. I walked to the back of the store, past the racks of magazines and videos arranged by orifice preferences. I stopped and looked into each one of the private viewing booths, that curious modern institution that engages the energies of the men who film the loops, the people who perform in them, the men who go into the booths and the men who clean up after.

All the booths were empty.

Another strikeout.

I left the store and walked back to the car with the dead man. There wasn't a person in sight. I knew people had heard the shots, but nobody seemed to give a damn. The most somebody would do was call 911.

I reached in and opened the driver's door from the inside. There was blood all over the dash, the inside of the windshield and the seat. It looked like a scene from a Chicago slaughterhouse during National Beef Week. Without moving the body or getting blood on me, I checked out the corpse and lifted the wallet from his rear pants pocket.

I wanted to take a look at the car's registration but I knew there wasn't going to be much time. Any second now a blue and white was going to be rounding the corner. I pushed the electric door lock and unlocked all the doors. Then I went around to the passenger door, opened it and reached in and popped open the glove compartment. I rooted around until I found the registration. I should have left it for the boys in blue, but they would know who the car was registered to and I wouldn't. The way I figured it, I needed it more than they did.

I didn't leave any prints. That would just confuse them.

The sirens sounded in the distance. They were coming from a couple of directions. I slammed the car door shut and double-timed it over to Second Avenue.

CHAPTER 26

According to the ID in his wallet, the dead man was a colonel in the Atlacatl Brigade of the Salvadoran army. Everybody was a colonel in that goddamn country.

His name was Luis Eduardo Navarette. He was forty-eight. Or he would have been in another month and a half, on February sixteenth. The card gave an address in the Escalon district of San Salvador. He had a platinum American Express card and a membership in one of those clubs called Flashdancers where big-breasted girls dance right in your face.

There was three hundred and fifty-six dollars in his wallet. That was the exquisite dilemma. I ruminated on it for a couple of minutes. Then I decided to send a check for three hundred and fifty-six dollars to the American Prostate Association, just in case.

I leaned back on my sofa and put my feet up on the coffee table. It was almost one in the morning. My stomach was starting to growl. I hadn't eaten anything since that pizza and beer for lunch. It was a question of eating something or hitting the sack.

It was too late to call Mrs. Roderick. I'd call her in the morning, but not too early. I got up and walked into the kitchen. I knew it was going to be slim pickings. I couldn't remember the last time I'd gone shopping. I took a look inside the refrigerator. There was a six-pack of Budweiser, or rather a five-pack. There was some out-dated yogurt and a jar of pickles. That was about it except for a plastic container of something I couldn't recognize. I tossed that out because I didn't know what the hell it was.

The freezer had a better selection. There were a couple of frozen pizzas and three frozen hot dogs. I didn't remember why or when I froze the hot dogs, because they keep for a long time in the refrigerator, but that's what I decided to eat.

There's an old unwritten law that says you shouldn't have pizza for two meals in a row. Besides, you should vary your diet because diversification is healthier. If I had pickles and beer with the hot dogs, that would be three food groups right there. Vegetables, meat and grains, if you consider the malt and hops and barley.

The next question was whether to boil or microwave the hot dogs. Microwaving was faster so that's what I did.

I ate the three hot dogs on a fork and washed them down with a couple of beers. After that I felt a lot better.

The registration had nothing to do with Colonel Navarette. The car was registered in the name of one Francisco Aviles who lived at One Seventeen East Fifty-seventh Street. The colonel was driving a car that belonged to somebody else. This Mister Aviles was going to be very irritated when he found out what a major cleaning job his car was going to require.

I put the ID and the car registration on the kitchen table side by side next to the can of beer. Where was the connection? What was the relationship between Atlacatl and anything else? Who were these people and what the hell did anything mean? Where was the satchel full of cash? Where was the fedora guy? It seemed like I was dealing with a gallery of ghosts. At least, on the Formica table in front of me, there were two pieces of paper that identified two specific human beings, one with a color photo of a man who was now officially a ghost. It was good to have something tangible at last, even if I had no idea where it would lead.

CHAPTER 27

"Who's handling that homicide on Twenty-fourth Street last night?"
I said.

Gene Black looked up from the papers on his desk. He didn't seem
overjoyed to see me. "I am, Rogan," he said. "What's it to you?"

I grinned at him. "Well, I'm going to make your day a whole lot
brighter. In fact, I'm going to illuminate your day like the fourth of
July."

"That's good because I can use some light."

He was right. He looked like he needed it. His eyes were more
tired than I remembered them. They were flat, emotionless, as if he'd
seen every kind of evil that man could perpetrate, and then some. He
must have been an innocent kid once, innocent and full of youthful
energy, but all that had been beaten out of him a long time ago. His
eyes said more than that. They said every expectation that something
good might happen had been reduced to odds that were as long as
winning the lottery.

His beer belly had gotten a little bigger and a little lower. He was
wearing a pink shirt, something a man should never do. And he had
on the wrong suspenders, the kind that clip on. He was one of those
guys whose five o'clock shadow shows up at noon.

But he was the best cop I ever knew.

"I can ID the shooter for you," I said.

His eyebrows went way up. "You just happened to be passing by the scene of the crime and now you're going to give me the guy that did it?" His voice was more raspy than ever from the relentless progression of cigarettes and booze.

"Even better than that," I said. I dropped the fedora on his desk. "This is his hat."

He pushed his swivel chair back from the metal desk. "Jesus, don't do that. It's bad luck." He picked up the hat carefully by the crown and put it on a chair next to him.

I shook my head. "It's only bad luck if you put it on a bed. You don't have any beds in this precinct house, do you?"

He squinted at me. "And how did you happen to be in that neighborhood at that time of night?"

"I was taking a constitutional," I said. "For my health."

He was skeptical. "In the middle of a snowstorm?"

"To each his own."

He shrugged. He knew he wasn't going to get much more than that.

"Any other eyewitnesses around there?" he asked.

"Just a hooker, that I saw. But I doubt you'll find her and, even if you did, she was so far gone she wouldn't have been able to recognize Bill Clinton with his pants down."

He turned back to his desk and started writing notes on a yellow legal pad.

"Bring me that good-looking girl with the Ident-I-Kit and the big tits and I'll give you a picture of him," I said.

He shook his head. "You're a dinosaur. We don't use that anymore. Everything is computerized now."

"Is that right? Then what happened to that cutie?"

"She got wise, stopped working, got married and had a baby."

"Smart girl," I said. "Traditional values, and all that."

"It sure beats taking endless sexual comments from these creeps," he nodded. "Now, I'll give you Moore. He'll work with you on the computer. When you get a likeness, come back here and see me."

"Why is that?"

"So you can tell me what you want."

"What makes you think I want anything?"

He squinted at me again. "When did you ever do anything for me without asking for a favor?"

"I'll save you some time," I said. "I want to know who the killer was."

"Any particular reason for wanting to know?"

I gave him a big grin. "I have a highly developed sense of curiosity."

He scrutinized me. "Is that all you want to know?"

"That's all I want from you."

It was his turn to grin. "And you don't even want to know who the dead guy was?"

The sonofabitch had me there. Caught me flatfooted. Was he guessing I knew who the stiff was because his wallet was missing or was he just playing that good old hard-nosed cop tune?

I shrugged. "That's what happens when you get old. Some parts get hard and some parts get soft."

CHAPTER 28

The apartment house where Francisco Aviles lived on East Fifty-seventh Street was a large expensive modern condo building. It was named the Galleria and it had every amenity known to man in the closing years of the twentieth century. There was a lot of glass and a lot of stone.

This was the kind of building that foreigners liked. They could buy an apartment without having to be approved by a co-op board. They could come and go without requiring approval from anybody and they could rent to whoever they chose. And the appearance was just flashy enough to appeal to them.

It was almost eight in the evening when I got there. Aviles had said over the phone he'd see me when I told him I was a friend of Colonel Navarette. Maybe he wanted to get some information on the Colonel's untimely check-out or maybe he just wondered who the hell I was.

Aviles' apartment was on the thirtieth floor. He opened the door to his apartment a couple of inches and looked out at me. Then he opened the door wide and said, "Please come in."

I stepped inside. Aviles was a tall man, almost as tall as me. He had fine features and cold blue eyes. His hair was short, neatly cut and graying. He wore glasses with round tortoise-shell frames. He was a distinguished-looking man, with the air of a senator who might have lent his name to reams of socially-progressive legislation.

"How do you come to know Colonel Navarette?" he said.

We stood in the vestibule of his apartment. His accent was thick, but his command of English was good.

"I was an American military advisor in El Salvador from nineteen eighty-one to eighty-three," I bluffed. It was impossible to be contradicted by a dead man unless Aviles had a direct line to Hell. "I was liaison officer to the Atlacatl brigade. That's where we met."

Aviles nodded.

He waved his hand back toward the living room.

"Come this way," he said. "Let me offer you a drink."

The apartment appeared to have been decorated by a professional. All the furniture and the decor and the colors seemed to match. It looked like it cost big bucks and it was in good taste. It wasn't the kind of decorating a guy would do by himself, and Aviles didn't seem to have a female in residence.

He looked at me. "May I offer you a Chivas Regal?"

Who was I to turn down such an offer? "On the rocks," I said.

He brought me the drink and held up his glass. "Health, love, money and the time to enjoy them," he said in Spanish.

"Cheers," I said. I took a drink. It was good.

He was wearing a cashmere jacket and a starched white shirt with a paisley ascot, something men stopped wearing here in the sixties. There was a disagreeable scent of cologne about him.

"I admired you and your compadres," he said. He sat down in what was obviously his favorite armchair facing the picture window displaying the lights of the Manhattan night. "Please have a seat."

I sat on the sofa in front of him.

"You were brave men," he said. "I remember you weren't allowed to carry M-16s, only sidearms. It was a foolish rule imposed on you by your civilian leaders. Simply a fig leaf in order to pretend you weren't engaged in combat. You were in harm's way with no means of defending yourself against the terrorists."

It was easy to see which side he was on. I wanted to ask him what his occupation was, but Colonel Navarette would have told me about Aviles before sending me to him, so I couldn't.

He must have read my thoughts, because he said, "I too was in the military for many years, retiring with the rank of colonel. But I was involuntarily demobilized and pensioned off, like some discarded piece of trash."

He took a deep swallow of his drink and let out a loud sigh. "If I sound bitter, you must forgive me. It's not often that I get the chance to complain to a fellow military officer."

"I understand how you feel," I said.

"We won that war and this is how we were rewarded." He raised his glass to me. "That is to say, your president, the great Ronald Reagan, won the war. He defeated the Soviet Union and, with that victory, he saved El Salvador, Nicaragua and Guatemala from the communists. When the flow of arms and funds from the communist bloc was cut off, the local insurgents had to rely on the Cuban supply and that was not enough to sustain them."

He raised his glass again to make a toast. "Here's to the great Ronald Reagan and to the valiant men who defeated the communist menace." He'd probably downed more than a couple before I showed up.

I held up my glass and took a big swig of scotch.

"Tell me, Mister Rogan, are you still in the military?"

I shook my head. "I decided to seek gainful employment in the civilian sector."

"Very commendable," he said. "And what is your civilian work?"

"I'm a private investigator."

"I see. And what are you presently investigating?"

"That's why I'm here, Senor Aviles."

He nodded. "I suspected as much. You require some information or assistance."

"That's right. I'm investigating the kidnapping of James Roderick in El Salvador. He was taken…"

He waved his hand. "I know the circumstances. An unfortunate occurrence. I didn't know the gentleman but I knew of him. He had a great reputation."

I finished my drink. Aviles refilled my glass in one smooth motion. "I'm here to find out if you know anything about the kidnapping or if you know someone who might."

He poured himself another one and stared out the window. He didn't say anything for a long time. Finally he turned to look at me.

"I have some sad news for you, Mister Rogan," he said. "Our mutual friend, Colonel Navarette, was murdered yesterday. He was shot to death on the streets of New York. The official police version is that this was a common crime of robbery but I do not believe it."

I tried to look surprised. "Christ almighty," I said, for want of any more profound words. "Yesterday, you say?"

He nodded, then pointed at me. "Since you are a private investigator and a friend of Colonel Navarette, I would like to engage you to investigate his murder and bring the killer to justice, in any way you must." He pointed at me again. "You understand what I'm saying, do you not?"

"Yeah, I understand, but as much as I'd like to help you, I can't. I already have a client and I'm working on that case full-time. I never work on more than one case at a time." He didn't know that was hogwash. I'd take as many cases as a hooker could take johns, or even more, since I didn't have to worry about running out of lubricating jelly.

He bought that. "I see."

"Let me ask you a question," I said with the proper amount of righteous indignation. "Who do you think killed Navarette?"

He thought for a minute. While he sat there silently, the smell of his foul cologne hit me again. It was musk.

A very musky musk. What kind of furry rodent would be sexually attracted by the scent of this musk? Maybe a capybara or maybe a muskrat. Certainly not a female of the human species.

"I have an idea of who did it," he said. "But at this moment I would prefer not to say. I believe it is someone who does not wish us well."

"What about Roderick, then?"

He nodded. "Yes," he said. "Don Jaime Roderick…" He turned his gaze out the window to the horizon and the lights of a cold night in December. The street noises were muffled and far below. "There is an American reporter in El Salvador by the name of McInerny."

"He's dead," I said.

He seemed surprised. "He was working on a story about the kidnapping. It is too bad he died. An accident, was it?"

"Sort of. He got in the way of a bullet."

"Most unfortunate," Aviles said.

What Aviles had just said gave me a thought. I could try to locate McInerny's notes and see if they contained anything that would be useful to me.

I got up. "Thanks for the information. And for the scotch."

"Sorry I could not give you more."

Did he mean the information or the scotch? I took one last look around the place and left. It sure was a luxurious setting for an ex-officer pensioned off by a third-world army. Too luxurious. Did this boy have another more unsavory source of income? Even old American soldiers didn't fade away in this lavish style.

Now for the enjoyable part of the case. I had to head south and locate a broad whose mission in life was to punch my ticket.

CHAPTER 29

I called Senora Roderick the next morning and brought her up to date, more or less. I didn't let her know that her money had gone into that giant sinkhole that's filled on a regular basis by PI's who aren't as smart as they think they are. I told her the case was progressing well, which was more than a slight exaggeration, since I didn't know where the hell it was going. And I told her I was going back to El Salvador to get her husband before it was too late and I hoped I sounded more convincing than I felt.

Then I called Broadbent at the U. S. embassy in Salvador and gave him a brief sketch of what had happened since we spoke. He didn't sound too confident either.

"I'm going to be taking a .38 and I don't want any problems," I said. "Get me clearance from customs."

"I'll do better than that. I'll meet your flight at the airport."

"And what about the widow McInerny? Did you get a fix on her?"

Broadbent misunderstood. He thought I was worried about getting ventilated. "We finally located the bitch. She's staying at a small hotel called Casa Austria. As far as we can tell, she's been quiet since you left Salvador. Don't sweat. We'll keep her out of your hair."

"Much obliged," I said. "I'll see you before the sun sets."

⚜   ⚜   ⚜

Broadbent met me at the airport in El Salvador and ushered me double-time through customs with his diplomatic pull. Nobody even checked my underwear. There was a black embassy Ford waiting at the curb with the engine running and the air-conditioning blasting.

I climbed into the car. Lightener was sitting in the back seat. It was a stretch job, so Lightener moved over to the jump seat to give Broadbent and me a chance to straighten out our legs.

On the way into San Salvador I filled them in on the details. Lightener had a little black notebook and he scribbled in it while I talked. Once a Company man, always a Company man. The Agency really trained their people well. Lightener was as methodical as he must have been when he was a spook. Broadbent was sweating like he had just finished running the marathon. He kept wiping his shaved head with his handkerchief even though the air-conditioning was working fine. His shirt was soaked through with sweat. Lightener, on the other hand, looked cool and comfortable and impeccable in his three-piece suit. From time to time he would smooth his thick black mustache as he listened. Finally I finished and we rode in silence the rest of the way into town.

Broadbent insisted I check into the Hotel Presidente in San Benito so the widow McInerny wouldn't know I was back in town. They dropped me off at the hotel and Broadbent said they'd pick me up in a half-hour to go to dinner.

I checked into the Presidente and followed the bellhop up to my room. After I'd showered and changed, I called the Camino Real to get the messages that had come in while I was away.

There were three messages. Two were from civilians answering the ad in La Prensa with information they hoped would put them on the road to riches. The other one was from Sister Angela. She left the number of a community house on the outskirts of San Salvador.

I called Sister Angela's number. An old man answered the phone and said he would take a message for her. He must have been almost illiterate because it took him a long time to write down my name and number. He made me repeat it several times to be sure he had it right.

Broadbent and Lightener took me to dinner at a Chinese restaurant but the food was barely edible. The dumplings were stuffed with some kind of petroleum-enriched silicone. After you've gotten used to eating in New York, the cuisine any place else is just passable, at best.

When we'd finished dinner, they invited me to go with them to some cat house to get our pipes cleaned, but I told them I had to go back to the hotel and wash my socks.

CHAPTER 30

After Broadbent and Lightener dropped me off at the hotel, I gave them a decent interval to get away and then went out front and stood under the awning. There was a solitary cab waiting at the end of the driveway. The driver was leaning against the car, grabbing a smoke. I called out to him. It was way past midnight. I wanted to check out this Casa Austria without their company.

The taxi driver took me to a middle-class neighborhood that was mostly newly-constructed houses. The lights were out in all the houses and the residents presumably tucked safely in bed. I told the driver to come back for me in an hour and paid him a handsome retainer and said there would be a lot more if he was punctual. There's nothing as uncomfortable as loitering in a good neighborhood after midnight without a valid reason for being there, except maybe for loitering in a lousy neighborhood.

The Casa Austria was a large private home that had been converted to a guest house. It looked like a clean and comfortable place from the outside. The streets were quiet and the only noises were a couple of dogs barking in the distance and the low whistle of the neighborhood watchman signaling that all was well. There were several street lights on the block and the trees on the sidewalk cast deep shadows on the pavement.

I walked around the block until I got back to the guest house. All the rooms were dark but there was a light over the entrance. I went up to the front door and tried it. It was locked. But it wasn't a tough lock.

The lock opened in less than a minute of working on it. The door swung open without any noise. I stepped inside and shut the door behind me. No way of knowing how soon the sereno would be making his rounds in front of the hotel. The entranceway was small. There was a light at the end of the corridor that gave a little illumination. On the right was a stairway. An antique desk was on the left.

I took a small flashlight from my pocket and ran it over the top of the desk. The only thing there was a ledger size leather-bound book. I opened the book and held the light on the page. It was the guest register.

The widow McInerny was in room 2C.

If the mountain wouldn't come to Rogan, Rogan would go to the mountain.

I went up the stairs slowly and made a right, because people always make a right turn. 2C was the second door on the right. The light was off under the door. There was one dim bulb in the hallway. The floors were tile so I tried to step without sounding like a herd of bull elephants. I stood against the wall at the top of the staircase. There wasn't a sound anywhere except for somebody snoring really loud from one of the rooms on the floor.

Next, I moved to the door of 2C and stood there with my back to the wall for a couple of minutes. The bulb overhead was so dim you could barely see to the end of the hallway. It was stifling. There was no breeze. The place needed a powerful air conditioner. I was sweating like I was playing volleyball in a sauna. I opened my top shirt button and loosened the bloody tie that was strangling me.

When I was sure that everything was secure I checked the door of 2C. It was locked but the lock was old. I worked it until it snapped open. I put my shoulder against the door and shoved but it wouldn't move. There must've been some kind of hook or catch. It took a couple of more shoves before it gave way.

I stopped and waited. It was quiet.

The door was open about two inches. I pushed it a little more. It moved with a loud squeak. I stopped. It was going to be better to open it all at once than get a series of loud squeaks. I waited. Everything was quiet.

I swung the door open a foot. There was another loud squeak and then silence. I didn't move for a full minute. The snoring continued down the hall.

It's written that a gentleman isn't supposed to be in a lady's bedchamber after midnight, but this was a special case. This was going to save somebody's life or get somebody killed. The room was dark, except for a thin shaft of moonlight that hit the floor next to the bed. I stepped inside and closed the door. As my eyes got used to the darkness, I could barely make out the figure on the bed. It was tough to see anything else.

I shone the flashlight around the floor, starting with my feet and then in widening circles. The bed was a meter and a half from my feet. Next to the bed was a night table.

There was a small foot rug by the bed. A dresser stood against the wall. That was all. The room was small, maybe four meters across.

I moved the light at waist level. There was a female form on the bed. That was all I could see. On the night table were four liquor bottles. They were bottles of Flor de Cana, the stuff that would stiffen you faster than a sack of concrete. One of them was lying on its side. There were also a bunch of pill bottles.

I walked over and studied her up and down. The broad sure appeared to be a boozer. I took another step until I was next to the night table. At the back of the night table was a small black gun. It looked like a Beretta. I took a closer look. It was the same piece she'd used to try to put a few holes in me in Roderick's concubine's store. I reached over and grabbed the gun and slipped it into my pocket.

I flashed the beam over the bed. The covers were down on the tile floor. The woman was on her back. She was wearing a T-shirt and panties. Her forearm was flung over her eyes. Her hair was blond and it was spread out all over the pillow. I moved next to the bed and put the light on her. The T-shirt had a large design on the front with the letters NPR and a picture of an old-fashioned microphone like the kind Frank Sinatra used to sing into. The panties were plain white cotton.

I grabbed her shoulder and shook it.

"Wake up," I said. "It's question and answer time."

She didn't move.

"Wake up, sister."

Still no sign of intelligent life.

I shook her again. This time she started to stir. She moved her arm away from her eyes. Then she slowly reached over for one of the bottles. Her eyes were still closed.

She groaned. It wasn't a pleasant sound. It sounded like a couple of boards being pried apart. Her hand smacked the bottle and knocked it off the table. It hit the floor and shattered. What a waste of some perfectly good rotgut.

"Rise and shine," I said.

She shook her head without opening her eyes and moaned. She was trying to say something but the words weren't intelligible. Her head kept moving back and forth.

"It's showtime," I said. "Time to fill in the blanks."

She grunted and this time she tried to open her eyes. It was a major effort. First she opened one eye and then the other.

"It's me." I smiled. I shone the light on my face and then back on hers. It must have been a real shock to her.

"Oh," she said. It took a few long slow seconds for the image of my face to travel the distance from her eyes to her brain. Then her eyes rolled back so you could see the whites and she blacked out.

CHAPTER 31

It took a full five minutes to bring her back. First I tried slapping her cheeks, but that didn't work. Then I took splashes of the rotgut and put it on her cheeks and her forehead. Pretty soon she started smelling like a distillery, but it didn't help. I did that for a couple of minutes. Then I took the pillow and the covers and wadded them up and put them under her feet.

After a while her eyelids started to flutter. I flicked on the light switch by the door. The overhead light was a single bulb but it did a good job of lighting the room. The place was simple but clean, aside from the broken glass and the spreading stain of alcohol on the floor. The whole room stunk of booze.

By now, the widow McInerny was back with the living. She wasn't sitting up yet, but her eyes were open and they were filled with fear. Her head moved slowly from side to side as she tried to survey her situation. She probably knew it wasn't good.

Before I could stop her, she made a quick move for the gun on the night table. She looked very unhappy when she discovered it wasn't there. She lay back down and turned to look at me.

I gave her another smile, a reassuring one. "I didn't kill your husband," I said.

She didn't look reassured. "What do you want?" Her voice was shaky.

"I'm not here to hurt you," I said.

She made an effort to sit up. "Why are you here?"

Her voice was a little steadier.

"I didn't kill your husband," I repeated.

She managed to raise herself up on one elbow. "I know," she said softly. She looked down.

"You do?"

She nodded. "Where's my gun?" she asked.

"You don't need that. It's going to get you in a world of trouble, especially if you don't know how to use it." I leaned a little closer to her. "Didn't your mother ever tell you it's bad manners to take potshots at a stranger in a brassiere shop?"

She flushed. It was tough to tell her age. She must have been in her late thirties, early forties. She appeared well worn. Her skin had the tired sheen that women get when they lose that dewy look.

"I wasn't trying to kill you," she said. She was sitting up now, but she didn't know what to do with her hands. She kept moving them nervously in her lap.

"How do you know I didn't kill your husband?" I asked her.

She looked over at the bottles of Flor de Cana on the night table. "I need a drink," she said. "I'm completely fucked up right now."

"Go ahead and ruin your health."

She slid over and grabbed the nearest bottle by the neck. It didn't matter which bottle she picked up. They were all open. She took a slug and then took one of the pill bottles and tapped out a pill and swallowed it with another slug of rotgut.

The booze must have bolstered her courage. She squinted up at me. "How did you get into my room?" she said. "And what are you doing here?"

"Is that one question or two?"

She was sweating and her hair was plastered to her forehead in strands. She shook her head and then reached up and brushed back her hair with her hand. As she reached up, those 36Cs strained against the microphone on her shirt.

"I didn't mean to hurt you," she said. She must have realized the precariousness of her situation. Who knew what this tall, dark and handsome stranger in her room was capable of?

"Relax," I said. "You don't have a thing to worry about. At least not from me. My job is getting into places I don't belong and asking a lot of questions."

"What are you? And what are you doing here?"

I grinned at her. "Looks like you're the one who's asking all the questions. That's my job, not yours."

She took another swallow of booze. "What is your job?"

"I have one job right now. That's to find a man named James Roderick. Does that name mean anything to you?"

She looked at me for a long time. "Why are you in my room?" she said finally.

"I'm a private investigator. That's what I do. I go into peoples' rooms in the middle of the night and scare the hell out of them."

"That's what you did to me, alright. You scared me shitless and I'm still scared and I'm not sure my medication is working." She took another slug of booze. "That medication is supposed to calm me down, and right now I'm not very calm. As a matter of fact, I'm very upset that you're in my room at night and you woke me up when you weren't supposed to."

"You can go back to sleep after you give me some answers," I said.

Her eyes narrowed. "Why should I help you?"

That was a good question, I had to admit. It took a couple of seconds to think of an answer. "Because I can help you."

She shook her head. "Help me? Exactly in which fucking way can you help me?"

"Don't you want to know who killed your husband?"

She stared at me. "Of course I do. What kind of a goddam wife would I be if I didn't."

I gave her my most winning smile. "I can help you find the men who did it."

She sounded skeptical. "How can you do that?"

"Because I was lucky and he wasn't. I was with him in that fire-fight when he bought it. They were shooting at both of us." I neglected to tell her I didn't have any better idea now of who ambushed us than I did then, except that now I believed it wasn't a random event.

"Why did they kill him?" she said. She let out a little sob. At least, it sounded like a sob. It could have been a hiccup.

That was my cue to jump in. "He was one hell of a guy," I said. "You had to admire him, the way he rounded up all that informa-tion. He said he wanted to write a story about me."

She rubbed her nose with the back of her hand. "Why you?"

I shrugged. "He said I made good copy."

She shot another glance up at me. She was obviously having a hard time deciding if she could trust me. She didn't speak for a while. Everything was very still. The sereno's low whistle sounded on the street outside the window. He might have noticed the light on in her room.

"How did you know I didn't kill him?" I asked her.

"He told me," she said flatly.

I blinked. "What?" Since when did corpses start to talk?

"I'm going to puke," she said. She put her hand over her mouth and got up from the bed on the side without the broken glass and ran barefoot across the room and out the door. I could've stopped her, I guess, but for some reason I didn't.

The door to the room was wide open. Down the hall in the bath-room she was retching loud enough to wake a drunken army. She kept hacking and retching until I thought she was going to cough up a lung. Then she stopped.

Now we had arrived at what is commonly called the Moment of Truth. Was she going to walk back into a room with a stranger who might harm her or would she stroll off into the night in her T-shirt and panties or would she just start to scream her head off?

How would you figure the odds? Three to one, one in three?

I waited what seemed a long time, but was actually less than two minutes. Then I heard footsteps padding down the hallway. She stepped into the room and shut the door behind her. She didn't look at me, but went and sat hunched down on the edge of the bed.

Good old solid citizen Rogan. She trusted me after all. Kind of gave a boost to my aura of professional competence.

"Sorry about that," she said. "Usually I can hold my liquor."

"And the pills go extremely well with the booze?"

She looked up at me sheepishly. "Yeah, I suppose that wasn't too healthy a cocktail." She got up and crawled across the bed on her hands and knees and grabbed a pack of Marlboros from the night table. She lit up a cigarette and exhaled slowly. "It's all right. I feel better now."

"Don't fret," I said. "I won't tell your parole officer."

She took a couple of puffs and blew them out in rapid succession.

"How did you know I didn't kill your husband?" I asked her again.

She nodded. "My husband was working on a story here that he hoped to freelance to some magazine. Either that or publish a book on the subject. Every couple of days he'd overnight me a disk by DHL with all the updates he'd written. On the next to the last disk, he mentioned you and that he thought you were somehow involved in the nasty business he was investigating."

She turned and eyed the Flor de Cana on the night table. She started to grab one of the bottles, but put it down without drinking any. Instead she sucked on the cigarette a couple of times. Then she started coughing as she exhaled.

"I received the last disk a week after he died, because he'd sent it by regular airmail," she said. "I didn't print it out until later."

"What did it say?"

"It was rather involved. I didn't fully understand it. He had apparently unearthed something about a cabal of ex-military officers who were involved in some nefarious scheme to use El Salvador as a transshipment point to smuggle copious quantities of drugs."

This babe talked like a walking thesaurus. I squinted at her. "What kind of work do you do?"

"I'm a reporter for National Public Radio."

I studied her face more closely. She looked like a cross between Cokie Roberts and Nina Totenberg.

"Oh, shit," I said.

"What's the matter? Don't you like NPR?"

I shook my head. "Too many long, boring, thumb-sucking pieces about agrarian reform in Central America."

"Well, that's what I do, whether you like it or not." She folded her arms across her chest. "Anyway, on the last disk, he said he was mistaken about you and that he didn't think you were part of the scheme. He said he thought you could help him and that he had some new information. He was going to take you to meet a contact he'd located."

I nodded. "Yeah, that was the driver of the man who was kidnapped, James Roderick. That was where we were ambushed. And that was where your husband was shot dead."

She couldn't restrain herself any more. She took a couple of swallows of the liquor. "What happened?" she said. "I mean, when he was shot."

"He drove me to the place. We were walking up to the house when they started shooting at us from both ends of the street. He took one of the first bullets in the head."

She held her head in her hands and rocked back and forth on the bed. "Oh, God," she said, her voice choking. "Oh my God."

I had a very strong urge to put my hand on her shoulder and comfort her but I decided not to. I just stood there and waited until she finished crying. It took a couple of minutes. She must have had a real case on McInerny. I couldn't help feeling envious, that a woman loved a man so much.

Finally she stopped and rubbed her eyes and took a deep breath.

"Do you have the disks here?" I asked her.

She nodded. "Yes."

"Let me take a look. Maybe I can make something out of them that you didn't see."

CHAPTER 32

"Hello, sleepyhead."

"Who is this?" I said.

It was after nine the next morning. I was still sacked out when the phone rang.

"This is Sister Angela," came the voice. "I'm calling you on the house phone. I'm downstairs in the lobby. Come on down."

"Give me ten minutes," I said.

She was sitting on a sofa staring at the carpet when I walked up to her. Her knees were close together and her hands were folded in her lap. She was wearing a white shirt and black slacks and sensible white nurse shoes with good arch support.

When she saw me, she stood up and gave me a firm short handshake. Once up and once down. "I have the person you wanted to meet," she said with her flat Massachusetts accent. She leaned in toward me and whispered, "You know, El Ciego, the blind one."

I nodded. "Good," I said. "When can I see him?"

"What about right now?"

"Outstanding," I said. "Lay on, MacDuff."

"What?"

"Never mind. Let's go."

She turned to look at me. "Are you still angry with me?"

"I was never angry with you. What you were doing was stupid and I told you so. You know you'll always get the truth from me—at least, the truth as I see it."

"Oh sure, behold the master of truth," she said with a nod and a note of sarcasm. She walked out of the hotel. I followed her. There was an old Ford truck waiting at the curb. It was a small flatbed without any uprights on the back. It had no markings and it carried no cargo.

She climbed into the driver's seat. I got into the seat next to her.

"Deja vu all over again," I said. "All we need is your factotum." She looked sideways at me.

"You can't talk until we're out of town," she said.

"Whose rule is that? Leon Trotsky's?"

She made a face at me and gunned the engine. We pulled out of the hotel driveway at an excessive rate of speed. For a nun, she had a very heavy foot on the accelerator.

We drove to the outskirts of San Salvador. When we were out of sight of any houses, she pulled over to the side of the road and stopped on a grassy patch out of the way of traffic.

"Are we there yet?" I said.

She shook her head. "I'm sorry. I have to take your gun."

"How do you know I have a gun?"

She smiled at her cleverness. "Because no one would wear a suit in this heat unless he wanted to cover over a holster and a gun."

"Smart girl," I said. I took off my jacket and tie, since she'd given me an excuse. Then I took off the holster and gun and gave them to her. She stuck them under her seat.

She hesitated.

"Well?" I said.

"There's one more thing I have to do."

"I hate to guess what that is," I said.

She shook her head. "No, I have to blindfold you so you can't see where we're going."

"That's pretty childish, isn't it?" I could just picture myself driving around the countryside with a kerchief over my face.

She gave me a half-embarrassed smile. "That's what they told me to do."

"Couldn't you pretend you did and tell them so?"

The look she gave me was the same as if I'd asked her to drive naked to Des Moines over the Pan American highway. "Oh, I couldn't lie to them," she said. "They trust me."

I shrugged. "Since you appeal to my better nature…"

She pulled out a flower-pattern cloth from her pants pocket and wrapped it around my face. It still had the faint odor of her body clinging to it. Better than nothing, I guess.

She shifted into low gear and we took off. At first, the roads were paved and the ride was fairly smooth. As we kept going, the ride got rougher and rougher. But that didn't slow us down. Not the nun on the Cannonball Run. We kept bouncing up and down in the cab of the truck like two jackrabbits in heat. We drove for more than an hour, maybe closer to two. It was tough to tell how long it took.

We didn't talk for a while. Then she broke the silence. Some people just have a congenital aversion to the absence of speech. She started telling me about her childhood in Massachusetts, growing up in a small town. About her boyfriend in high school, both of them shy and innocent. She said she was still innocent, but not so shy anymore. She told me of her rebellion against her religious upbringing and the strictures of the parochial schools. And of her epiphany and conversion in the face of the death of her boyfriend and her own near-death experience. She said her faith was stronger now than ever and that it was manifested by the desire to protect and support the downtrodden of the world against the depredations of the money-grubbing capitalists.

It sounded like the same old song, enlivened only by the ferocity of her words and her obvious sincerity. It was actually a strange experience, bouncing up and down, sucking in all that dust on an empty stomach, without being able to see a damn thing and listening to the communist manifesto spoken by a girl with a Massachusetts accent. Disorienting, really.

I didn't say much. Just grunted assent now and then. If you want to know the truth, I liked listening to her talk. It helped pass the time.

She started shifting gears more frequently and making right and left turns, so I knew we were getting close. Then she slowed down and said, "You can take off your blindfold now."

"Where are we?" I said.

She laughed. "After all that trouble with the blindfold, and now you ask me that?"

"Can I have my gun back?"

She didn't even bother to answer that one. She just giggled and whacked my chest with the back of her hand. She shifted into low and urged the truck up a steep incline.

We were in a heavily-wooded area on the side of a hill. The truck strained and rocked back and forth over a rutted ditch as it tried to make the grade. It was tough going.

It took a good ten minutes, but we finally made it over a rise and pulled into a small clearing. There were two rustic huts with tin roofs in the middle of the clearing.

Some men were squatting around a pile of wooden crates, a stack of ancient rifles on the ground next to them. There were two mangy horses without saddles tied to a tree at the edge of the clearing. A thin plume of smoke came from the roof of one of the huts. The door was open and you could see a woman making tortillas over an open stove, her hands slapping the dough back and forth. Two bare-ass kids ran in and out of the hut, making squealing noises as they played tag.

The men who were squatting got up and waved at Sister Angela as we drove into the clearing. There wasn't even a road, just a dirt path that we rode over. There were seven men in all. They were wearing tattered olive drab uniforms. The whole place had a bad smell, as if it was sitting on an open sewer.

Sister Angela got out of the truck and walked over to the men. They talked for a few minutes. Then she came back to the truck and said to me, "These men will take you to meet El Ciego. I'll give them your gun. They'll give it back to you after your meeting and they'll see that you get a ride back to San Salvador."

I climbed down from the truck. "Thanks," I said.

She looked square into my eyes. "I've done my part of the deal," she said. "Now will you let me take care of my business without any trouble?"

I shrugged. "You can do what you like. I was just talking to you like a Dutch uncle."

"Dutch uncle or not, I don't need your advice."

"Fair enough," I said. "But you should know that people fall all over each other and pay large sums of money just to get my advice."

She rolled her eyes at me by way of farewell. "Take care of yourself," she said. "You're much too nice to be in this line of work."

"So are you," I said.

CHAPTER 33

Two rebels separated themselves from their comrades and came up to me. Their rifles were slung over their shoulders with the muzzles pointing down. They motioned for me to follow them.

We fell into single file as we left the clearing and headed into the woods. I walked between them. There wasn't even a path to follow, as far as I could tell. We walked for fifteen minutes, more or less, until we got to another, smaller clearing on the side of the hill. This one didn't even have a hut, just a fire pit with some boulders in a circle around it. There was nothing else in the clearing.

We stood there waiting. After a couple of minutes, six guerrillas came out of the woods. Five of them were wearing the same ratty olive drab uniforms. The sixth man had a new, neatly-pressed uniform. He was taller than the others. He had a full beard that was turning gray and eyes that looked far beyond me. He walked haltingly, holding a cane in one hand and the arm of the man next to him with the other. The men walked up to me.

The blind man extended his hand in my direction. "Mister Rogan," he said. His English was unaccented.

"You know my name?"

"That's not all I know."

I took his hand and shook it. "What's your name?" I asked.

"You know my name," he said. "As a matter of fact, you've met my uncle. A most disagreeable fellow, wouldn't you say?"

Something buried away in my memory came back. A story about a boy burned in a fire. Blinded and crippled. Hoag's story of greed, revenge and a blood feud. It had to do with an essential oil called Balsamo de Peru and a combination in restraint of trade. A dying man's deathbed request to his brother to avenge a wrong done to the family. It sounded like the stuff of operas.

"Well, I'll be damned," I said. "You're Dieter Strassberg's nephew." There was a momentary vision of a metal-working factory in the heart of the jungle with steam and flames rising from the ovens like a fiendish depiction of purgatory. And one son of a bitch who still had my treasured Glock.

"A brilliant deduction," he said. "No wonder you're highly paid as a private detective."

"Not so highly paid," I said to set the record straight. "But tell me one thing. If you were a card-carrying member of the privileged class, why did you become a revolutionary? You had everything you wanted, and then some."

He gave me a small smile. "There is such a thing as idealism. I won't try to explain it to you, since I know your mindset. Suffice it to say that I felt a need to better the lot of the poor people of this country."

"Then why didn't you do it through the system?" I asked him, even though I knew the answer before he said it.

He sighed. "When I started this life ten years ago, the non-violent way wasn't possible," he said with a note of sadness. "Now, perhaps…" He spread his hands in front of him, the cane in his right hand. "But now it's too late for me."

"No amnesty?"

"Not for me," he said. "There's too much blood on my hands. They want me to pay for my sins."

I took a look around at the rebels and then back at El Ciego. "Your English is very good for a guerrilla," I said.

"How kind of you to notice. I was educated in the States, actually, and graduated from Tulane. So I'm quite familiar with your culture and all its flaws."

"You're making a value judgment based on your prejudices. You're supposed to be value-neutral."

He snorted. "That doesn't apply in my case since my profession depends on my prejudices."

There was no use wasting time. I got to the point. "The reason I wanted to see you is that I'm trying to locate a man named Jaime Roderick. I was informed you had information as to where he was being held."

"You were partly misinformed. I have a pretty good idea of who kidnapped him and the circumstances of his captivity, but I have no information concerning his whereabouts."

"OK," I said. "Why don't you tell me what you do know."

He started to turn in the direction of the boulders. "It's difficult for me to stand too long. My leg, you know. Do you mind if we sit?" Without waiting for an answer, he moved with the man supporting him over to the largest rock and sat on it.

I walked over and sat on a big rock next to him.

"Your friend was held in a room dug in the ground, with a dirt floor, cinderblock walls and wooden boards for a ceiling."

It didn't sound like a room with too many amenities. "How do you know?" I said.

He shrugged. "Because that's the way it's always done."

"And who took him?"

He moved his cane from side to side. "From what I've heard, a group of ex-military officers. But I could be wrong."

"You don't think the Left has him?"

"I would have heard if they did. And I've heard nothing. Besides, you're using the wrong tense."

I was starting to get a bad feeling. "What do you mean?" I asked.

"You're using the present tense. I used the past tense."

I didn't like the way that sounded. "You mean he's dead?"

"That's what I've heard. But that's only a rumor circulating among the revolutionaries, for what it's worth to you."

"Was he killed?"

He shook his head. "I don't believe so. The word is that he died of a weak heart, because he lacked his medicine."

"You said he was taken by military officers…"

"Ex-military officers," he corrected me.

"And why did they do it?"

"Look at it this way," he said. "Imagine you're a colonel in the army, living high on the hog. Your word is law. You're a demi-god. You can get as much money as you want through bribery, corruption and extortion. Then imagine the war comes to an end. You are surplus. Unnecessary baggage. Under the peace accord, the army must reduce their ranks. You're unwanted and unneeded." He ran his fingers over his beard, smoothing it out.

"Now think of a man who had so much power and money reduced to the status of pensioner. A few colones a month income. Stripped of his power and influence. Shunned by those politicians who once courted his favor. Oh, how the mighty have fallen. Ozymandias, King of Kings."

He attempted a smile in my direction.

"So these ex-colonels decided to pick up some loose change by kidnapping wealthy businessmen and collecting ransom money," I said.

"Precisely. You must understand that times are hard now and there are few employment opportunities available for men who have practiced the profession of violence all their lives."

"And these ex-officers pooled their talents and split the proceeds?"

"That is correct," he said. "And the reason they kidnapped wealthy businessmen is that these people have the liquid funds."

"Very cute," I said. What this guy said was starting to make sense. "But there's one thing. I made a payoff in New York. Why didn't they release Roderick?"

He laughed. He was probably enjoying the delicious irony of big bucks passing from one dirty pocket to another.

"Why should they? Your client was already dead. What good would that have done?"

I couldn't answer that one.

"Do you…" I stopped talking.

There was a big hole in El Ciego's forehead.

Then I heard the shot.

I hit the deck. Specks of his brain and skull were all over my shirt.

Then all hell broke loose. I looked up the side of the hill and saw puffs of smoke where the sniper was located. I rolled behind a boulder for cover. It looked like the clearing was taking incoming from all sides. The rebels were shouting and running for cover as the rounds kicked up dirt all around us.

One guerilla was hit in the back as he made for the boulders and the force turned him around before he went down with a grunt. That left six.

They gathered in the fire pit with me, shooting back at an unseen enemy with their rifles and sidearms. It was an uneven contest. The firepower pounding us was overwhelming. The noise sounded like a jackhammer was in the hole with us, working on overdrive. The smell of gunpowder made it tough to breathe. Everybody was shouting and coughing. It was total confusion and then some.

Then they remembered me. This uninvited stranger in the hole with them. The cause of all their present discomfort.

"I will kill this son of a whore," one of the rebels shouted. He lowered his rifle and pointed it at my chest.

It wasn't exactly the most cordial situation I'd ever been in. Matter of fact, it was pretty grim. My stomach tightened up like a dried pig's bladder.

The guy next to him knocked his rifle away with the butt of his own. "Let him live," he said. "If he is alive, he may be our way out. If he is dead, they will kill all of us."

"Good thinking," I said. "Let me be your meal ticket."

They gave me a blank look. Maybe they didn't know what a meal ticket was.

Another volley took out one more rebel. A slug caught him in the neck as he stuck his head up for a better look and the blood sprayed out all over the place like an oil gusher. He flapped his arms up and down as the life ran out of his body. It didn't take long.

There were five guerrillas in the pit with me. We were hunkered down behind the boulders, wishing the pit was deeper and the rocks were bigger. But it wasn't bad cover. If we kept our heads down, it would be tough to dislodge us. We had good fields of fire in all directions around the clearing.

The rebels started shooting back whenever somebody tried to enter the clearing. From time to time they'd hit one of the soldiers who was dumb enough to expose himself to fire by crawling across the open grass. They were still pouring heavy fire on us but it wasn't doing much damage. There wasn't anything I could do. I just huddled up in a ball with my arms over my head, trying to make myself very small and very inconspicuous.

The situation was a stalemate for the moment. The clearing was a free-fire zone that no one could enter. We couldn't move out and the government troops around us couldn't move in. The rebels with me had enough ammo to last them for a while. The men on both sides kept firing at each other without any real effect. There was automatic and semi-automatic fire, but nothing heavier than that. The heaviest piece sounded like a Browning Automatic Rifle from the government side. The army's rounds kept ricocheting off the boulders around us, making a big racket but doing no damage. From time to time, the government troops would loose some heavy bursts and then lapse into desultory fire.

There was no change for the next twenty minutes. Then some heavy firing started coming from the south. The incoming fire from that direction stopped. It looked like the soldiers to the south of us were taking fire from their rear.

A shout went up from the men with me. It appeared that a relief column of rebels from lower down on the mountain had caught the government soldiers from behind and had them pinned down in enfilading fire. The men around me poured all their gunfire down the hill against the soldiers' position. The government troops were taking a heavy pounding from both sides.

Minute by minute, the battle changed. There was now a big hole in the army's line and the rebels had turned the army's flank and were rolling it up. It wouldn't be long before the men in the pit would be able to break out. The government soldiers were retreating along their line in an orderly manner, covering each other. But they were retreating.

The leader of the men with me, the one who'd stopped the other guy from decorating the fire pit with my guts, started yelling at the men to get ready to make a run for it. He asked for a volunteer to stay behind and put down covering fire so the others could get out. Never mind that he was asking the poor sucker to commit suicide. A small sacrifice in the grand revolutionary scheme of things.

One guy did actually volunteer. You had to be impressed. It reminded me of those other small dark tenacious and fearless soldiers who fought the greatest army in the world to a standstill with their wooden punji stakes half a world away.

"We will take this dog with us to protect us from their fire," the leader said. There was no dog with us, so I guess they were referring to me. The men grabbed up their ammo and weapons and crouched behind the boulders, ready to make a run for it.

"Now!" the leader shouted. He stuck his rifle into my left side and said, "You go first. I will be right behind you."

Ordinarily I would've attempted to discuss the subject with him in a measured and thoughtful manner, but this didn't seem to be the most auspicious moment. Everybody was hot with blood lust and the line, "Come let us reason together," didn't have the right ring to it.

Reluctantly, I got into a low crouch and slid between two rocks and exited the relative safety of the fire pit. Actually, more than anything else in the world right now, I just wanted to stay in that hole that had become home.

"Run, dog," the leader said.

I did.

I crouched as low as I could and ran as fast as I could in the direction of the rebel soldiers toward the south. The rounds hit the grass all around me. I didn't turn around to see if the men were following me. My eyes were fixed straight ahead at the safety of the tree line. I couldn't hear a damn thing because the firing was so loud.

Then I heard rotors. Instinctively, I turned to look. Rising up from below the tree line were two Huey gunships in formation, like two giant dragonflies. The wash from the blades blew the grass and everything else in the clearing. The gunships opened fire with TOW wire-guided missiles on the hole in the government line that the rebels were trying to fill. It was unmitigated slaughter. The rebels fell like grass under a lawnmower. There was no contest. Their small arms fire was too ineffectual to do any damage.

I hit the ground and just tried to become part of it. There was no place to hide. I wanted to pull the ground up over me. The rebels with me did the same. We couldn't run and we couldn't stay.

The gunships made another pass over the clearing, firing as they went. To the south, the rebels had fallen back into the cover of the jungle. The government troops started filtering back to close the hole in the line that the rebels had briefly held. The contest was over.

We stayed where we were. The firing had lessened. There was some occasional small arms fire but it wasn't the hot battle it had been minutes earlier. The choppers took a stationary hovering position over the clearing.

It was a moment suspended in time. Nothing moved. If not for the noise of the choppers and the wash of the rotors, it would have been as peaceful as an oil painting of a summertime afternoon.

Then the choppers gradually lowered themselves until they were positioned a few feet off the ground. Government troops jumped out in groups of twos and threes. We didn't move. Our faces nuzzled the dirt like we loved it and wanted to become part of it.

Then a lone figure hopped out of the nearest Huey. He started walking toward us. The swaggering gait was familiar. So were the sunglasses. It was Colonel Mayorga. He came toward us like a bantam cock of the walk, grinning from ear to ear over his victory.

When he got about ten paces from us, he pulled out a forty-five and put a slug into the back of the head of the first rebel on the ground in front of him. The other men jumped up and started running like hell. I did the same.

Mayorga got off two more shots that hit two men in the back. They both went down.

There were two guerillas left. One of them was the leader. The soldiers closed around us in a ring, their rifles leveled at us.

"Drop your weapons," a soldier yelled.

The rebels did. They raised their hands.

"Do not kill them," Mayorga said, with his lisp. "We need information."

"Si, senor," the commanding officer said. The soldiers edged in on the guerillas. They grabbed the rebels' hands and pulled them behind their backs and tied their thumbs together with bailing wire.

Mayorga swaggered up to me. He clapped his hand on my shoulder. "Muchas gracias, Senor Rogan," he said. "I have the honor to extend the deepest appreciation of the government and the armed forces of El Salvador for your invaluable assistance." He let out a big guffaw. "You're one hell of a jarhead. Fuckin' A. You nailed that cocksucker for us, while we've been trying to track him down for years. Let me shake that hand of yours."

He extended his hand to me.

I hauled back and nailed him with a right cross to the jaw that sent him flying through the air and left him sprawled on his ass. He was a lot shorter than me, so maybe it wasn't strictly fair, but Jack Kennedy always said that life was unfair, and he wasn't the first man to say it. Maybe the ancient Greeks were.

Mayorga got up, rubbing his jaw. He wasn't grinning any more. "Hey, man. Why the hell you do that?"

"Take one guess why, you bastard," I said.

CHAPTER 34

"Do you have access to a computer?" I asked Marta.

She made an unpleasant face. "I do not believe in computers. Computers are black magic. They are the creation of the devil."

"Interesting concept," I said. "Do you know whose computer I can use?"

She looked around her living room and thought for a minute. "If you wish, you can use Antonio's. I have seen several in the offices."

"I'll call him."

"Do not bother. I am going to his house for lunch. You can come with me."

It wasn't a bad offer, as offers go. But I was hoping for a better one. Back into the honeypot, for example. I leaned over and kissed her. Her reaction was distinctly lukewarm.

"You're not randy?"

She shook her head. "No, I'm not feeling randy at the moment."

"Any particular reason?"

She looked right through me. "I heard what you did to El Ciego. That was not very noble of you."

I shrugged. How does one respond to a remark like that? I always thought I was noble, but I guess some people could see it differently. "Let's go to Antonio's," I said.

It took two minutes for the chauffeur to drive us over to Antonio's house. We could have walked it in less than five minutes, but physical exertion was not a way of life for the upper classes in the tropics. Antonio's house was almost as opulent as his father's, but it was built in a more traditional Spanish style. It was a huge house for a single man to live in alone. And evidently, he lived alone. At least his sister and her mother shared their house when they were in El Salvador.

Antonio met us at the door. He had a small grin on his face. It was the first time I'd seen him smile. Every other time he was either bawling or on the verge of bawling.

"Congratulations, Senor Rogan," he said. He shook my hand with a limp grip that felt like a moist flounder. "All the world is talking about how you tracked down El Ciego. You are the hero of the country."

"Hero to the free-marketeers," I said.

His grin broadened. "Nevertheless, you are welcome in my house. Please enter."

We went in. It was cooler inside the house. The midday sun was getting past the point where it made any sense to be outdoors. The furnishings were meager and non-descript, almost threadbare. Less expensive than you'd expect, given size of the trust fund this lucky sperm must have.

We sat in the living room and drank iced Margaritas, served by little ladies in starched white dresses. It wasn't half bad. You could get used to a life like this.

"What news do you have of our father?" Antonio asked.

I told them what had happened, at least as much as I thought they should know. Then I explained why I needed access to a computer, but I didn't tell them where or how I came by the disk.

"I believe he was taken by a gang of demobilized military officers," I ended up saying. I didn't mention the rumor that their father was dead.

Antonio's eyes brightened. "Do you have any idea where they are holding him?"

I shook my head.

Marta was not very talkative. Antonio did most of the talking for the two of them. He seemed overjoyed because of what had happened in the jungle, although I couldn't see what the hell that had to do with him.

"This is a wonderful victory for our class," Antonio said, raising his Margarita. "We must drink a toast to it."

His comments finally pushed Marta past the tick-off point. Her skin reddened more than its usual freckle-faced ruddiness. "You are a fool," she said to Antonio in Spanish. "When you talk about our class, please do not include me. I do not wish to be part of your class."

Antonio flashed her a nasty smirk. "It's very simple then. You can give up your comfortable existence and your inheritance and go to live among the peasants. Let us see how well you do without your Gucci and your Hermes."

"That is easy to say. You never had to work for your money. Everything was given to you. Expensive cars. Big houses. Without Papa you would not be Managing Director. You would be Assistant Janitor."

Antonio bit his lip. The guy was about to lose his composure. His baby sister sure had the knack for bringing him close to tears. His sallow complexion took on the look of parchment stretched taut.

"Where can I use a computer?" I broke in.

Antonio let out a long sigh. "Let us eat lunch first," he said. "Then you can come to the office with me and I will see that you have a private place to work."

The lunch was health food. Tofu, avocados, plantains, papaya and mangos. No creature that had eyes. And flan for desert, that shapeless, tasteless, quivering mass. You had to feel so damn robust after eating a meal like that. It gave me a terrific craving for a rare steak.

During the meal the conversation ranged from problems with the servants to the onerous duties on the importation of luxury cars to the most exclusive locations to vacation in Europe.

Then it was siesta time. Marta said she was going home to nap. Antonio offered me a guest bedroom.

I shook my head. "I never got into the habit," I said.

"Very well," Antonio said. "Then you can watch CNN, if you like. I take a short nap, only a half-hour. Then we can go to the office."

"Fine with me," I said.

He took me to a sparsely-furnished room and sat me down in front of a large-screen TV. The maid brought a tray of cold beers and set them down next to me, together with a bowl of chips. There was a remote on the sofa. I turned on CNN and watched some inconsequential soft feature about pollution in Antarctica. It wasn't long before I nodded off.

So much for never getting into the habit.

❦   ❦   ❦

Antonio had a corner office in a decrepit building adjoining a warehouse in the old center of San Salvador. From his window, you could see the loading dock and the parking lot filled with delivery trucks. There was a putrid smell of industrial waste that permeated the entire area.

He led me down a dimly-lit corridor past a warren of tiny rooms to a windowless office with a table and chair. On the table was an old AST 286 with a small black and white monitor.

"If there is anything you require, please let me know," he said.

"What about a computer from the twentieth century?"

He gave me a sheepish look and spread his hands. "Unfortunately, this is all we have available at the moment. I hope it will suit your needs."

"It's probably OK," I said. "I think there's just text."

Antonio left the room. I slipped in McInerny's disk, switched to the A drive, and watched it come up on the screen.

The disk contained a rough draft of a long article or a short book, interspersed with McInerny's comments and footnotes. The man was a professional. He'd really done his homework. You had to be impressed by the effort that had gone into it.

Not only did it come complete with names and cross-connections, like an organizational chart, it even had extensive historical background to show how this group had come into existence.

It took more than an hour to read through the text.

There was a section on the group's connections with current members of the military. One of the familiar names, together with his military record, was our buddy Colonel Mayorga. And, according to McInerny, the leaders of this sterling group were two men I'd already had the pleasure of meeting. One of them had just gone to see his maker while I looked on. That was the guy who was shot in the Lincoln Town car in New York, one Colonel Navarette who, since he was recently deceased, would find it difficult to hold any kind of leadership position. The other boss was Colonel Aviles, who owned the Lincoln Town car that Navarette was killed in and who lived in that penthouse in the Galleria on East Fifty-seventh Street and who was in love with Ronald Reagan.

But the part that interested me most was a program that used El Salvador as a transshipment point to smuggle cocaine from Colombia to the States in barrels of Balsamo de Peru. The report said that since President Noriega's untimely downfall, Panama had lost its value as a transshipment point because the DEA had come down hard on the Panamanians and they couldn't go to the bathroom without written permission, let alone open a bank account. As far as the cash generated from this project was concerned, McInerny wrote that it was laundered through a one-office bank in Miami named Metrobank that was located in a strip mall in the suburbs.

The plan involved wrapping the coke in watertight packages attached to the inside of the barrels of Balsamo and duping the local Swiss laboratory that certified the integrity of the seal on the drums. I recalled that Hoag had told the story about the three men who had monopolized the export of Balsamo de Peru. One of the men was Roderick. The other man was Strassberg's dead brother, El Ciego's father. Who was the third man?

Did this scheme have anything to do with Roderick's kidnapping? Did he find out about the coke smuggling and threaten to blow the whistle? Was that crime just a little too far over the edge for Roderick? Or did he revert to type and have a fight with his partners?

I leaned back in the chair and put my feet up on the table. The last page on the screen told about how he'd come across an American detective who claimed to be trying to find a wealthy man named James Roderick who had just been kidnapped, but that he didn't believe this lowlife. The private investigator, a guy by the name of Edward Rogan, seemed to be hiding something, but he wasn't sure what. McInerny put in his notes that he was going to tail this Rogan and find out what the hell he was up to.

It's a strange feeling to be reading a dead man's comments about you. It's like sitting on the crapper in a stall while your officemates discuss your shortcomings without knowing you're there. It isn't an occurrence that takes place very often.

But then something must have happened to make McInerny change his mind. The final paragraph said that he thought maybe Rogan was a straight shooter after all and that he was going to take Rogan to try to locate Roderick's chauffeur in Santa Tecla.

Vindication, at last. Even if it had to come from beyond the great divide.

CHAPTER 35

I was in my room washing up for dinner when the phone rang.

It was Mrs. Roderick calling from New York.

"Mister Rogan, Mister Rogan," she screamed. She said something I couldn't make out. She was breathless, almost hysterical. It was unlike her.

"Calm down, Mrs. Roderick. I can't understand you."

I could hear her take a deep breath on the other end.

"Mister Rogan, please. I have just received another ransom letter in my post office box." She was trying hard to keep her voice even. "I am very afraid."

"Do you have a fax?" I asked her.

"What?"

"A facsimile machine."

I could hear her take another breath. "Oh, yes. I have one."

"Good. I want you to fax me the note. I'll call the service desk and get the fax number downstairs. Are you at home?"

"Yes," she said.

"I'll call you in a minute. Wait for my call."

I got the hotel fax number and called her back with it.

Then I went down to the reception desk and waited until the fax came in. The clerk pulled it out of the machine and walked over to me, scanning it as he approached.

"Interesting reading?" I asked him.

He handed it to me like it was a leper's diaper. "I am so sorry, senor. Please forgive me. I did not mean to be discourteous."

"Forget it," I said.

The fax had the same typeface as the other two. But there was something different about it.

YOU FILTHY WHORE.

WE ARE READY TO COLLECT OUR MONEY. PAY NOW OR YOUR SON OF A WHORE HUSBAND DIES. WE WILL CALL YOU TOMORROW.

ATLACATL.

The note was closer in tone to the first ransom note she showed me in my office in New York. Now I knew what was going on. The second note was written by someone else. Somebody who had knowledge of the first note. Somebody who picked up the money that I let get away. The first guy had Roderick. The second guy had the payment.

And I was looking more like an asshole every day.

※   ※   ※

There was a group of people waiting in the hotel lobby to get into the restaurant for dinner. I walked past them on my way toward the front entrance to meet my driver. Broadbent and Lightener had called and left a message asking me to eat with them. As I crossed the lobby, I saw a woman get up from a sofa and stand blocking my path.

It was Sister Angela.

At first I didn't recognize her because she was wearing a dress. A long dark dress. Her face was pale. I couldn't make out the look in her eyes. They were dull, glassy, bloodshot. It looked like she had been crying.

She just stood without moving or saying anything.

Then she finally got out the words. "You're a bad man. You're a terrible person. You're evil."

She stood there and pounded on my chest with the sides of her clenched hands. "You're horrible."

"I hate you," she sobbed. "I hate you so much." Tears formed in her eyes and made them glisten. She kept pounding on my chest with those little hands like a child.

I stood there and didn't say anything.

I was a foot taller than her and weighed a hundred pounds more than her.

But it still hurt.

CHAPTER 36

At dinner, I told Broadbent and Lightener what I'd picked up so far. I didn't tell them what I thought. They both sat quietly, taking notes. From time to time, Lightener would smooth down his dark slicked hair or his mustache. Occasionally he'd ask a question. They didn't seem overly impressed. Lightener suggested I go to a lunch meeting of the Salvadoran-American Chamber of Commerce the next day at the Camino Real. He said I'd meet a man by the name of Warren who might have information on Roderick.

After they dropped me back at the hotel, I called the Czarina.

"Don't do anything," I told her. "Just take the information and stall them."

She seemed hesitant. "What if something happens to my husband?"

"Do it my way."

"As you wish," she said finally.

It was a risk, I knew. But I reasoned this way. If the rumor was true, Roderick was dead already. If he was still alive, they weren't going to kill him now. And the odds were he wasn't going to die in the next couple of days. It was like Pascal's wager, only with a more immediate payoff.

Just after I hung up on Mrs. Roderick, the phone rang. I thought she was calling me back to ask another question, but it was Gene Black calling from the precinct.

"You're not working banker's hours, Lieutenant," I said. It was ten PM in El Salvador, so it was eleven PM in New York.

"Hell, I'm still on duty from yesterday. I tell you, retirement's starting to look better and better."

"You get your shooter?"

"Almost as good," he said.

"What do you mean?"

"I know who he is. The only problem is finding him."

"Why?"

"He doesn't exist anymore."

"Why not?" I asked.

"He used to be a CIA agent in good standing. Now he's been disavowed. The Agency has no idea where the hell he is or what identity he's taken. He's gone out of their control. All they know is that he's not who he used to be or where he's supposed to be and probably never will be again."

"That a fact?" I said. It was going to take some time to digest that one. "What about the license plate I gave you?"

"No luck. We couldn't match it with anything. Too many possibles."

"Thanks anyway. Take care."

"Wait, Rogan," Black said. "Before you hang up…"

"Yeah?"

"We tracked down the owner of the Town Car that guy was killed in. Turns out he was some kind of Colonel in the Salvadoran army. That a surprise to you?"

"Why?"

"Because the dead guy was a Colonel in the Salvadoran army too."

"Yeah, so?"

"Well, I got something else that might surprise you," Black said.

"What's that?"

"The owner of the car in question, one Colonel Aviles, was whacked with one slug to the back of the head in his apartment in the Galleria the day after you left New York. It looks like that Town Car was bad luck all around. What do you make of that?"

I was surprised. Another promising avenue leading to a dead end. "Christ," I said.

"And by a curious coincidence, you just happen to be in El Salvador as we speak. May I ask you a dumb question? What the fuck is going on?"

"I'll tell you when I see you," I said.

"And when, pray tell, is that going to be?"

"When I pull a guy out of a hole in the ground."

❦   ❦   ❦

At eight-thirty the next morning I decided to play a hunch. Usually my hunches didn't work at the Meadowlands, but this time I felt lucky.

I put in a call to the Metrobank in Miami.

The operator answered.

"I want to talk to Mr. Lightener."

"I'm sorry, Sir. Mr. Lightener is not currently available. He's out of the country."

"Is he in El Salvador?"

"I'm sorry, Sir. We're not allowed to say where he is."

"Thanks anyway, Sugar," I said. "Your lack of assistance has been invaluable."

And to tell you the truth, it was more than invaluable.

CHAPTER 37

Marta frowned. The lady didn't like being woken at the crack of dawn, which in her case was ten in the morning. She swept into the sunlit living room still wearing her nightgown. It was a flimsy white job with a lot of lace. She rubbed her eyes as she walked up to me. Her wild red hair was even wilder when it was uncombed.

"Why do you come around so early?" she said.

"I have a few unanswered questions."

"Always questions." She rubbed her nose with the back of her hand. "Why do you think I can answer your questions?"

"You talk to a lot of people. You just might pick up some information in the course of your conversations."

She shrugged. "Very well. You can try to ask me some questions. But I am not sure I can help you."

I watched her closely. It was probably too early in the morning for her to be devious. "Did your father have any connections with the military or the CIA?"

Her eyes went up and to the left as she thought. She didn't answer right away. "I can not think of any connection. You know, there are many parts of his business he does not tell me about."

"This doesn't necessarily have to do with his business," I said. "It could be personal or even not directly connected to the business."

"Please?"

"What I mean is, did he talk to anybody that would make you suspicious?"

She stared at me. Finally she said, "I can not think so early in the morning. I must have coffee."

She called for a pot of coffee and said, "Come on. Let us sit outside on the patio. It is so much more pleasant."

She led me through a set of large sliding glass doors to a sitting area looking out over the lawn. It was still cool outside. In the distance a gardener in a wide-brimmed straw hat was hunched over, trimming the lawn with a machete. You could hear the rhythmic swoosh, swoosh as his blade sliced through the grass and you could smell the freshly-cut grass.

"Did your father have any contact with anybody in the army or the CIA?" I repeated.

Marta waited while the maid put the tray with coffee and cups on a small table and then said, "I do not think so. He was totally concerned with his business. Anything else did not interest him." The coffee was in a French press. She pushed the knob on top down slowly until all the grounds were at the bottom of the pot. She poured two cups and took a sip of coffee. "He did have some conversations with a man from your United States drug agency. He told me he was helping this man."

"The DEA? The Drug Enforcement Administration?"

She nodded. "Yes. I believe so."

"Do you know what they talked about?"

She shook her head. "I didn't know and I didn't care. It was a matter of indifference to me. I don't take drugs and therefore I had no interest. You could talk to Antonio. He worked closely every day with our father. He might be able to give you more information." She glanced up at me. "Do you think the drug agency kidnapped him?"

"No," I said. "He was probably working with them. Maybe trying to stop drug smuggling. That may have been why he was taken."

She sniffed. "You do not know my father. He would not do anything to help someone unless he made money from it. He was not interested in charity."

"Maybe they were paying him," I said.

That seemed to intrigue her. She screwed up her face in contemplation. "What would my father know about drugs?"

I told her the story Hoag had told me about her father's part in the combination to restrict the export of Balsamo de Peru and the connection with El Ciego. Then I told her about McInerny's report on the coke smuggling in the barrels of Balsamo. Then I tied the package together for her with a neat red ribbon.

Her eyes widened, but I wasn't sure if it was because of the story or the caffeine. "I have heard people talking of this, but I never believed it before," she said.

"You can believe it. I think your father's kidnapping was tied in with this coke business. Either he was running cocaine or he was trying to stop it. So it comes down to a simple question of good or evil. Was your father a good man or a bad man?"

Few children have had so direct a question put to them. She had to stop and consider. I could see she was struggling with the answer. It must have been an illuminating moment for her. She lit up a Gaulois and puffed on it hard a couple of times. Finally she narrowed her eyes and said, "I do not think I want to answer your question."

"Why the reticence all of a sudden?" I said. "You never missed a chance to badmouth your father before."

"This is different. This is serious. This may be a crime. If he does not come back alive, I do not want to be the one to blacken his name forever."

"Don't concern yourself," I said. "You've already answered my question."

Her eyes censured me. "You are always so ready to think the worst of everyone. You think everyone is bad."

This broad was extending the range and extent of my cynicism a little too far. I shook my head. "Oh, no, sweetheart," I said. "You got it wrong. The world is ninety-nine and forty-four one hundredths percent pure. For starters, I think your mother is a good person. I believe her."

She stood up and put her hands on her hips. "You think you are so smart, but you do not know anything. You are tall and handsome and stupid. You do not even know why my mother hired you, do you?"

This was going to be good.

"Why don't you tell me."

"Yes, I will tell you," she said softly, drawing in her breath. "You think my mother is so pure. You think she cries because she loves my father and misses him. But the real reason she wants him back alive is so that she can persuade him to change his testament."

"His will?"

"Yes, that's right. His will."

That got my attention. I leaned forward. "Sit down," I said.

She sat down.

"How does his will read?" I said.

She smiled. It was an unpleasant smile. "You would like to know this," she said. "My father made a new testament several months ago. He made many changes. He left almost all of his money to his filthy concubine. He left the business to Antonio. And he gave very little, almost nothing, to me and my mother." Her smile had disappeared. "So now you know why my mother wants him back."

I looked deep into those lovely eyes.

"And now I know why you hate him so much," I said.

✿   ✿   ✿

I took a cab to Hoag's place. I didn't want to use Lightener's driver. There was no telling what kind of goodies the driver was passing back to the employer who put bread on his table.

Hoag walked down the front steps to meet me. Apparently he felt secure enough on that quiet tree-lined street to venture out of his house. He towered over his uniformed bodyguards like a sequoia over the pines. He was wearing the same kind of pale blue guayabera with white embroidery that he wore the last time I saw him.

He grabbed me in a giant bear-hug.

"Senor Rogan," he said in his booming middle-European accent. "What a pleasant surprise to see you so soon. Now you can carry the gift to the young lady in Miami that I spoke to you about."

"Sure thing. There's just a little information I need and then I'll be your personal package service."

"Wonderful, wonderful," he said. He wrapped his large paw around my shoulder. "I said that you would not be here long, didn't I. Come inside. Be my guest."

He took me into the house, then out to the patio where we sat the last time. The same little old Nina served us the same old Turkish coffee. I had an overpowering sense of having done this before, maybe because I had.

"What do you know about a man named Lightener?" I said.

Hoag nodded and stroked his walrus mustache. "Very rich and very powerful. But do not get on his bad side. He will show you no mercy."

"What about his background?"

"He is norteamericano. He worked for your CIA for many years. Then he married a girl from one of the fourteen families and took the family wealth and made it much larger. Some people say his business methods are not honest."

"Does he have any connection with Balsamo de Peru?"

Hoag nodded. "His company exports Balsamo."

"What's his connection with a bank in Miami called Metrobank?"

He smiled. "You are very good, Senor Rogan. Most people do not know this. It is not officially published anywhere, but Lightener is an owner of this Metrobank."

"What are the odds that the bank is washing money from drug smuggling?" I said.

Hoag leaned toward me. He lowered his voice. "One hears things. The odds may be good." He leaned back in his seat. "What does this have to do with Balsamo?"

"What if I said there was an operation to transship cocaine from Colombia in barrels of Balsamo? Would…"

Hoag let out a low whistle. "I have heard that some military officers were carrying out such a plan. But what does this have to do with Senor Lightener?"

"That's what I'm going to find out." I looked at him. "Do you know Lightener's girlfriend?"

He nodded. "Yes."

"Where does she live?"

"Why do you ask this question?"

"You should know as well as anyone," I said. "Always follow the snatch."

CHAPTER 38

It was a couple of minutes after noon when I got to the Camino Real. I asked at the front desk for the Salvadoran—American Chamber of Commerce luncheon. A bellhop showed me the way to a large conference room with a wall of picture windows that opened out onto the garden in front. Beyond the flowers and the lawn you could see the traffic on the main thoroughfare. The midday sun shone in through the big windows and covered the room with a blazing light that made the air-conditioning struggle overtime. The air-conditioning was losing the battle. The meeting hadn't started yet. Men in dark suits were standing in small groups drinking and talking and nodding in agreement. There wasn't a female in sight.

I asked around for the man named Warren that Lightener had referred me to, but the answer I got was that he hadn't arrived yet. So I decided it was time for a cold one. I took the Suprema and wandered about the room, searching for someone I knew. Nobody looked familiar. Lightener and Broadbent weren't there. The men standing around the tables and the bar were fairly evenly divided between gringos and Salvadorans.

About twelve-twenty a man on the dais called the meeting to order. I sat down at the nearest table next to a clean-shaven balding man of about fifty with bad teeth and deep wrinkles around his eyes. He said hello so I returned the greeting. We shook hands. He said he was the controller of a paint manufacturer. I told him I was a tourist, here to enjoy the waters.

The speeches started. It was the usual flow of hot air having to do with the joys of free enterprise and the amity between the United States and El Salvador. My mind kept drifting off to the connection between Lightener and the ex-military officers and Roderick's kidnapping. I couldn't see the relationship.

What if Lightener was in competition with the officers? He'd want to shut down their operation any way he could. Suppose he sent me in to locate them? Once he knew who they were, he could have had the top guys knocked off in New York. But who the hell kidnapped Roderick? And did it have anything to do with this coke business?

The waiter appeared at my shoulder and asked if I wanted the chicken or the fish. I'd eaten so much chicken on this trip that it would have almost been second-nature to want to screw a rooster. I ordered the fish. The waiter took a step back to his station and wrote down the orders. He double-checked his pad, then he nodded to himself and went out to the kitchen.

I glanced out the window. Some clouds had drifted by and obscured the sun. A Hummer was pulling into the hotel driveway. It started to pick up speed. It rolled up the curb, over the lawn and through the flower garden. It was going really fast now. Then it turned abruptly. The sonofabitch was heading straight for the plate glass windows in front of us. As it came, time slowed down and stopped ticking off seconds.

"Jesus Christ," I said.

The Hummer crashed through the wall of glass. Shards of the windowpane went flying through the air like a slow-mo kaleidoscope. The Hummer rolled over a couple of tables before it stopped in the middle of the room. Four guys jumped out. They were wearing civilian clothes and bandanas over their faces. One guy pulled the pin of a grenade and tossed it onto the floor. They retreated behind the vehicle for cover and started firing bursts from their automatic rifles into the ceiling.

I didn't wait for a hand-delivered invitation. I dove behind the waiter's station with my back to it, hunched over and closed my eyes and covered my ears. The exit was five meters in front of me.

The grenade went off with a huge noise and a brilliant flash. I knew what it was. A concussion grenade. The people in the room screamed in panic. They staggered around the room, blinded, deafened and stunned.

Exactly what the bastards wanted.

I got down on the floor and snuck a look out from behind the station. The guys were striding around the room, their weapons at order arms, looking for something.

Or someone.

I pulled back, then stuck my head out again and took a quick look at the guy nearest me. He was holding what looked like an AR-15. The bastard looked familiar behind the bandana. I'd seen him before.

Then I remembered where.

Right in this same goddam hotel. He was Armando. Lightener's bodyguard. The guy who lent me his tie.

The tie that contrasted with the sophisticated fashion statement I was trying to present and made me look like Joe Six-Pack.

I dropped back behind the waiter's station and pulled out my .38. The people were still screaming but the guys had stopped firing their weapons. I looked out again and took aim at this Armando and was about to squeeze one off when a guy behind me yelled, "Look out. There he is."

I hadn't seen him.

He fired a burst that tore off the top of the waiter's station.

I rolled back in his direction and took a shot at him. It missed but it made him lose his balance and fall back onto the floor. I glanced in the other direction. A man next to me had been hit by some of the rounds. Most of his face had been blown off. He had no eyes or nose. Only a part of his jaw was intact. He wasn't moving.

I looked around, trying to spot Armando. He wasn't anywhere I could see. Everyone was in a general state of agitation. It was time to depart this scene before they could do any more damage.

I got into a crouch and started for the rear exit, pulling off a shot over the head of that bastard who'd fallen. That kept him on the ground for another couple of seconds. It was enough time for me to make the door. In the process I had to step over a couple of men who were curled up in a fetal position on the floor, hoping this wasn't the day they were going to that great big businessman's luncheon in the sky.

CHAPTER 39

Lightener's girlfriend's house was located in the Colonia Escalon at the end of a cul-de-sac. I got there in a taxi I'd picked up at Metro Centro across the street from the hotel. Lightener's Mercedes was parked in front of the house with the engine running and the chauffeur deep in slumberland. It didn't look like any of his bodyguards were around.

I told the taxi driver to pull up on the other side of the street. We waited there for fifteen minutes without seeing anything. It was a quiet lower-middle-class neighborhood with well-kept little houses and neat lawns. The houses had little flower gardens in front and hanging baskets with orchids trailing down.

Some kids were playing a running and jumping game a couple of doors down and their laughter sounded across the early afternoon streets. It reminded you of a more innocent time when the important things were less important.

After a while Lightener emerged from the house across the street and shut the door behind him. He hunched over and locked the door twice with two keys, as if he was protecting his most prized possession. He moved slowly, dreamlike. He seemed older and there was a weightiness in his step. He turned and moved away from the door.

I got out of the taxi and crossed the street toward him. There was no traffic. Matter of fact, there hadn't been a moving car on the street in all the time I'd been waiting. I got within ten meters of Lightener before I yelled out to him. He hadn't even seen me.

"Lightener, I want to talk to you."

He blinked in surprise. A flash of fear and rage moved across his eyes. Perhaps a sudden realization that the game wasn't playing out the way he had planned it. I wasn't supposed to be standing where I was, interrupting his pleasant afternoon schedule.

Then Lightener said, "Rogan, you…"

He reached inside his suit jacket with an abrupt motion. But his timing was off. After a man has pumped out his ejaculate, a certain lassitude comes over him. It slows him down. Maybe it was just the smallest fraction of a second, but it was enough to give me the advantage. Out came his gun. He tried to steady his aim. His grip was shaky. He seemed to have trouble with the safety. I had my weapon out at the same time he did. I got my shot off just before his. The slug hit him square in the chest. The impact deflected his aim.

His shot went wide.

The sonofabitch was finished. He wouldn't be killing anybody for a very long time.

CHAPTER 40

Broadbent pulled the Ford up to the curb in front of the hotel. "Get in," he said. "There's something I want to show you."

I climbed in and sat next to him. "You heard about Lightener?"

He nodded. His face was grim. "Tell me exactly what happened." He put the car in gear and we rolled out of the driveway and into traffic.

I laid it out for him by the numbers. About the competition for the drug trade with the ex-military officers, the killings in New York, the money-laundering through the bank in Miami, the thugs in the Hummer trying to whack me. When I was finished, he took his eyes off the road and turned toward me and said, "That's all fine and good, but where the hell is Roderick? And where's the money?"

"I don't know, but you can make book I'm going to find out real soon."

He nodded again but didn't say anything. We drove for a while without talking. Broadbent kept gunning the engine and taking chances on the curves. He headed out of town toward Santa Tecla, then took a left turn in the direction of the coast. We drove past women on the side of the road hawking watermelons, the insides split open to display the red pulpy ripeness.

"Where are we going?" I said.

"To La Libertad," he said, his eyes straight ahead.

"Why?"

He didn't answer for a minute. "You'll see," he said.

La Libertad was the old port of San Salvador. Now superseded by the new port of Acajutla, it was a sleepy dusty town where nothing much happened. I had no idea what was there but, knowing Broadbent, this was going to be worth seeing.

The road narrowed as we started to descend to sea level. It would have been charitable to describe it as a two-lane highway. The other side of the road hugged the wall of the mountain and our lane fell away in a steep decline. There was no barrier on the outside of the lane.

Broadbent always drove too fast. I remembered that.

The oncoming traffic brushed by the side of the Ford and forced us closer to the edge. It was a ten or twenty meter drop to the next level and then another long fall to the bottom of the valley below that. But Broadbent had good control of the car and drove like he knew the road.

As we swung around a curve, he glanced at me out of the corner of his eye. "That Marta's a wicked-looking number," he said. "Hot little cunt, she is. Did you slip it to her?"

"What?"

"You give her the high hard one?"

I hesitated. There was a part of that old-fashioned gentleman in me that still thought discretion was a quality to be valued. "Yeah," I said finally. Then I realized why he asked. "You're the swordsman. Unless I miss my guess, you were in there too. Am I right?"

He turned to grin at me. "Yeah. I was in like Flynn. But only once. You know why?"

I shook my head. "Because you didn't meet her exacting standards for performance?"

He guffawed. "No, no," he said. "I heard this from other suckers like you and me." And then he tapped me on the knee. "Because she only fucks you once, and then she discards you like a used scumbag."

I shook my head. "That a fact?" I said. "Well, at least it's better than humping a black widow."

"Why's that?"

"Because a black widow kills you after she mates with you."

*   *   *

We drove for another ten minutes. Then Broadbent leaned forward and swiveled his gaze to survey the road front and back. The sunlight glinted off his shaved head like a high beam as he turned to look. He slowed down and pulled off the road onto a small grassy space that was just big enough to hold the car.

"What's up?" I said.

"I have to take a leak," he said. He climbed out of the car and took a couple of steps to where the ground fell away in a steep rocky incline and lowered himself over the edge.

I couldn't see where he'd gone to relieve himself. But I could hear his stream as he pissed on what sounded like a large flat rock. He took a long time to finish.

There wasn't much traffic going by at this hour of the afternoon. Probably siesta time all across the land. The air was heavy, humid and dusty. It felt like you could grab large chunks of it with your bare hands.

I considered whether or not to get out of the car. Broadbent would probably be back in a minute. So I sat there and pondered the eternal verities that had guided civilizations since the dawn of time.

It wasn't too long before Broadbent climbed back up to where we were parked. Only now he was holding something in his hand that he didn't have before, and it wasn't his dick. It was a big black forty-five automatic. And he was pointing it right at me.

I wasn't very surprised.

"Don't tell me you're pissed off because I fucked your girlfriend," I said.

He didn't laugh. He didn't even crack a smile.

"Where's your celebrated sense of humor?" I said.

He shook his head. "End of the road," he said. "Move over." He pointed with the muzzle to the driver's seat.

"My license is expired," I said. "It's against the law for me to drive."

He begrudged me a small smile. "You'll be expired, all right. Now get behind the wheel."

In a way, it was what I wanted. But not exactly this way. It was pretty clear Broadbent was hooked up with Lightener. Two superannuated cold war veterans with enlarged prostates and no enemy to fight anymore. The problem was proving it. There was no direct evidence and they were both such competent spooks, the odds were good I'd never be able to tie them together. Broadbent knew I was coming after him, so he took a preemptive step to stop me before I got there. And I held his hand and let him take me for a stroll down that primrose path.

I slid over to the driver's seat and looked out at him. His eyes were very small. "What's the drill?" I said.

He nodded at the cliff. "You're going over."

"And if I don't choose to?"

His eyes got smaller. "I'll put a big hole in your head right now."

I nodded. "That's not a very appetizing choice."

"Hobson's choice," he said. "No choice."

I tried to give him an innocuous look. After all, this was a dive I wasn't particularly eager to take. "What if I say let's forget the whole thing and I'll go back to New York and take up ballet and needlepoint and haute couture. You can go on with your business and I'll make believe this never happened and pretend we're still friends."

He shook his head. "Not a chance. I know you. You're a relentless bastard. You never stop." He held the gun out in front of him and squinted along the barrel. "It's time for you to go over."

I considered the options. There were few. I could reach for my gun, but my head would probably be blown away before I even got to it. I could respond like Bartleby the Scrivener—I prefer not to. But that would also just lead to the loss of my head, something I preferred to keep intact, if at all possible. And he was too far away for me to grab the gun from him.

"Put it in gear," he yelled.

He didn't say which gear, so I put it in reverse. As I jammed the accelerator, I ducked my head as low as I could and turned the wheel away from him as far as it would go. I heard a shot. The tires squealed as the car broadsided him with a loud thump. The car spun around and ended up facing the road.

My heart was pounding against my rib cage so hard I thought I was hit. Sweat was rolling down my face and the back of my neck. The sweat stung my eyes and made me blink. I pulled out my gun and looked around.

I couldn't see him.

I opened the door slowly and got out of the car. He wasn't anywhere I could see. I took a short walk around the car. I squatted and looked under the car.

There was no sign of him anywhere I looked. This guy was better than Houdini. I walked over to the road and looked in both directions. He'd really disappeared.

I went back to the car and leaned against the trunk, trying to figure out what a semi-articulate private dick does when a killer vanishes. It wasn't very tough to figure out. He goes to the edge of the incline and sneaks a peek over.

Broadbent was lying on an outcropping of rock about ten meters below me. He was still. His body was twisted like a contortionist. His eyes were open but blood was oozing out of his nose and mouth. The gun was on the ground about three or four meters from him, stark black against the brownish-green grass.

I climbed down slowly, grabbing hold of the rocks and bushes as I descended. When I got to him, I could see his back was probably broken. Nobody's back could bend at that kind of angle. His mouth was moving but there was no sound coming out. I bent down and moved my hand over the smoothness at the back of his shaved scalp.

His head was split wide open. I put my finger inside and touched something soft and wet. It was a raw gaping wound. Blood was flowing from the opening in his skull and collecting in a pool in the rock under his head. At the rate he was loosing blood, he wasn't going to be present very much longer.

I took off my jacket and folded it and put it under his head. I had another suit of the same color that could use an extra pair of pants.

"You don't have a lot of time," I said.

He nodded weakly. It took a lot of effort.

"You were partners with Lightener?" I said.

"Yeah," he whispered.

"Lightener had the money and the business cover to move the cocaine. You had the CIA contacts to get it at the source. Right?"

He didn't nod. He didn't have the strength. "Right," he said softly.

"Where's Roderick?"

"I don't know." I could barely hear him. His life was taking leave of his body. I moved closer to him.

"You have the ransom money?"

His eyes fluttered. "Yeah."

"Where is it?"

"In my apartment in Washington."

"You wrote the second ransom note?"

He sighed. His breath was coming harder. "Yeah."

"Who wrote the first ransom note?"

"I don't know," he said.

"Who kidnapped Roderick?"

He blinked a couple of times. "I don't know."

"Is Roderick alive or dead?"

He choked. He was drowning in his own blood. He could barely get the words out. "I don't know."

"What is Atlacatl?"

His eyes went sightless.

Then he was gone.

There was nothing more I could do for him. I climbed back up to the road and began the long ride back to San Salvador.

CHAPTER 41

"Where's your father?" I said.

Antonio glanced up from the papers on his desk. It took a long minute for my question to register. His eyes were bloodshot. "He is dead," he said in a low voice. He looked down at the desk. Then he started to cry softly.

He covered his face with his hands. They were trembling.

"It wasn't a kidnapping, was it?"

He shook his head. "How did you know?"

"Because you were the only one who spoke well of your father. Everybody else hated his guts. And you looked like you were as poor as a churchmouse. I figured he kept you on a tight leash. You couldn't wait till he was dead and gone so you could collect your money and take over the operation."

"He would tease me. He would say he would live until a hundred and twenty and I would never have the business. He never gave me a centavo. I had to beg for it. And that whore, my stepmother, would always take his side. I hated him. And I hated her because she could never replace my beloved mother."

"Where's your father's body?"

His voice choked up. "My men buried him in a shallow grave near La Palma. I saw it. It is just a small mound of dirt."

"What is Atlacatl?" I asked.

He shook his head in dismissal. "It means nothing. It was just a name I took from a history book. It has no significance."

His hand reached down to open a desk drawer. "Please let me do the correct thing," he sobbed.

I stepped around behind the desk and opened the drawer and took out the gun.

"You're obviously not cut out for this line of work," I told him. "That's not the correct thing."

There had been enough dying today.

I grabbed his arm and pulled him to his feet. "Let's take a walk." You can be sure you wouldn't want to be in his place. A jail cell in El Salvador could be a mighty unpleasant residence if you planned to spend a number of years there.

But then again, with all his money, he might be able to buy his way out of his punishment and spend the rest of his years sunning himself on the French Riviera.

It made very little difference to me.

CHAPTER 42

On the flight back to the States, I considered the two jobs I had to do. One was fairly pleasant and the other was distinctly unpleasant.

I had to stop off in Miami and deliver the gift from Hoag to his girlfriend. A token of affection. People still had clandestine affairs. People could still feel emotions. Maybe the present would make her happy.

Then I had to inform the Czarina that she wasn't going to get the money under Roderick's will. That would make her unhappy. She'd get back the ransom money, but that was simply a return of her own principal and wouldn't even be a small fraction of what she'd been expecting. In the United States, she'd have had a decent chance of contesting the will, but in Latin America she was considered little more than chattel and her legal recourses were few. A dead man's emotions would change the life of a woman who ran a small lingerie store in a shopping mall and make her a very rich woman.

Fortune's wheel had turned once more.

It was too late for lunch and too early for dinner.

I was tired. I didn't feel like having a drink so I closed my eyes and took a long nap.

THE END

About the Author

Gerald J. Davis was born and raised in New York City. He has hitch-hiked through seventeen countries in Europe and Asia and has lived in Central America. He has worked as a film editor, bellhop, stock-broker, lab technician, librarian, advertising executive and financial planner. He holds a Master of Science degree in Finance. He is the author of seven novels and is currently writing his eighth book.

He is married and has a son and a daughter.

His e-mail address is **gjdwriter@yahoo.com**.

0-595-23579-4

Printed in the United States
22766LVS00003B/223